Hazzard's Head

Scott Sommer

POSEIDON PRESS
New York

This novel is a work of fiction. Names, characters, places and incidents are either the product of the author's imagination or are used fictitiously. Any resemblance to actual events or locales or persons, living or dead, is entirely coincidental.

Library of Congress Cataloging-in-Publication Data

Sommer, Scott.
  Hazzard's Head
  I. Title
PS3569.O6533H39 1985   813'.54   85-12257
ISBN: 0-671-55678-9

The author gratefully acknowledges permission to reprint the following excerpts from previously published material:
page 25: *The Art of Loving*, pp. 94–94, Erich Fromm, Vol. 9 in *World Perspectives*, planned and edited by Ruth Nanda Amshen. Copyright © 1956 by Erich Fromm. Reprinted by permission of Harper & Row Publishers, Inc. *(Continued on page 193)*

For Harvey Hirsch
and in memoriam
Harrigan, the Irish terrier,
September 4, 1969–October 25, 1983

Driven by daemonic, chthonic
Powers. And right action is freedom
From past and future also.
For most of us, this is the aim
Never here to be realized;
Who are only undefeated
Because we have gone on trying. . . .

—T. S. Eliot

Endure that toil of growing up;
The ignominy of boyhood; the distress
Of boyhood changing into man;
The unfinished man and his pain
Brought face to face with his own clumsiness. . . .

—W. B. Yeats

We already know that neuroses are a result of repression,
not of events themselves.

—Alice Miller

THE INHABITANTS OF HAZZARD'S HEAD

Mother	Boy	Writer	Son	Punk
Father	Actor		Recluse	Paranoid
Teacher	Patient		Lover	Depressive

Part One

One

"*H*ELLO, *darling. I am returned from Rome now. I miss you and want to fuck with you. I love you so much still. Call me. Ciao.*"

Now in winter, hearing again her words in his head as snow fell softly upon the city, Jack Hazzard woke at dawn to darkness. All thirteen of the inhabitants of his head woke now on the twenty-eighth of December in his one bed where, though there were thirteen of him, he lay alone, thinking of Marcelline Tatia, from whom, until last night, he had been safely separated by the Atlantic.

Hazzard had terminated the Lover's one-year affair with Marcelline seven weeks ago, before she'd returned abruptly to Rome. Actually, after six months of psychoanalysis, it was the Patient in him who had inspired the breakup.

Naturally, many of the inhabitants had been unhappy with Hazzard's decision. The Lover, for example, along with the Punk, Boy, Depressive and Actor, each had responded with antipathy to his decision. But the Teacher, Mother, Father,

Recluse and Paranoid were unequivocally supportive (although for different reasons). The Son had not voiced an opinion: in his sexual shame he remained vividly silent. For the Writer's part, he did not engage personally in the conflicts which impoverished and exhausted the inhabitants of Hazzard's Head (each of whom, in different ways and in different situations, were either in contradiction to or at variance with each other). Indeed, the Writer merely manipulates the myriad neurotic conflicts of Jack Hazzard to amuse himself and make a marginal amount of money. In other words, though *in him,* to the Writer Jack Hazzard is simply one more character in his fictional world.

Consequently, the Paranoid believes the Writer to be a vindictive and hateful presence in Hazzard's Head. He believes the Writer's fundamental and exclusive intention is to humiliate those inhabitants whom he, the Writer, considers personally responsible for the unhappiness that created him. The Paranoid, therefore, is afraid of the Writer, that he might reveal things about Hazzard for which he, the Paranoid, will be punished. For that matter, all the inhabitants of Hazzard's Head, save the Teacher, are afraid of the Writer (and each other, of course), for they were created (like the Writer) to protect Jack Hazzard from himself.

The Teacher is another matter.

Frankly, the inveterate conflicts of the inhabitants of Hazzard's Head intensified with such virulence during the first months of the Lover's affair with Marcelline Tatia that a majority of the inhabitants acceded to the Paranoid's admonitions that the disintegration of Jack Hazzard's personality was imminent. Thus was the Patient created in their thirtieth year of being Jack Hazzard.

Yet now in winter, during the lonely week between Christmas and New Year's Day, it was the obsessive Lover who tormented the Patient at dawn by replaying Marcelline's message, left the previous evening on the telephone-answering machine:

"Hello, darling. I am returned from Rome now. I miss you and want to fuck with you. I love you so much still. Call me. Ciao."

TWO

NAKED, Hazzard rose from bed into the cold and foundered down the darkened corridor to the bathroom, where the Patient stored his cache of pharmaceuticals. Staring skeptically at himself in the mirror-fronted medicine cabinet, the Depressive in Hazzard ingested two Ludiomil antidepressants while the Paranoid popped a Valium to bridle the anxiety generated by the conflicting reactions of the Patient and the Lover to Marcelline's message.

"Fuck with me is right!" muttered the Paranoid in him, as Hazzard threw back his head to swallow the pills. Alas, after only seven weeks of separation from Marcelline (a separation soberly mandated by the Patient), the Lover confessed now in Hazzard's Head, "I still need her; I love her." "Your ass I love her," said the Punk, "I hate the bitch." "Just make up your minds already," said the Actor, "because I can't play two conflicting roles at once." "I can," said the Depressive wryly. "We did with Mom and Dad," put in the Son and the Boy percipiently.

The shower's cascade of hot water catapulted steam

throughout the room, and Hazzard watched as his mirrored image deformed before disappearing completely. Then he went beneath the warming water, closed his eyes and raised his face to the thrusting streams. He pictured her perfectly now, and his hand stroked slowly until his shaft straightened.

She was petite, with slender shapely legs and long auburn hair, which she parted in the middle and hooked behind her ears. Her gray-blue eyes, moted heavily with black liner, imparted an admixture of arrogance and nubile vulnerability that the Actor considered fetching; and her nose was small, "a cute girl's nose," thought the Lover; yet her mouth, thin and heavily lipsticked, suggested a severity that frightened the Son, Boy and Paranoid. Of course, the Punk's focus of judgment was informed by more prurient criteria: he dug the bitch for her sculpted, ample ass and those firm little breasts with their turgid nipples.

Italian, and twice divorced at thirty-seven, Marcelline considered her arrangement with Hazzard an "affair." She was "his mistress"; he "her lover." Hazzard, however, American, and seven years younger than she, preferred to think of their erotic manipulations as "a relationship."

Their last time together had been an unseasonably sultry Halloween evening; and with the windows flung wide open, Hazzard and Marcelline had sat side by side, drinking vodka in celebration of their first anniversary together. She had worn a black leather skirt and high heels and had been braless beneath a beige button-up cashmere top. Upon the worn Oriental rug at her feet lay a plastic bag which, Hazzard had presumed, contained certain "personal" artifacts for the weekend.

"Did you bring the stockings?" he had asked, leaning in to kiss her neck as the vodka he'd been drinking finally kicked in to erase his inhibitions.

"I'm wearing them."

He had whispered then, touching her pendulous earrings with his lips, "I don't feel.. . ."

"With the garters you love so much!"

Hazzard's right hand had slid slowly higher to feel the straps on her thighs, her leather skirt sighing as it slid upon the stockings.

"I want you to keep on the heels," he had told her, his lips upon her neck as his hand played under the skirt.

"What else do you want, darling?"

She had looked at him languorously then, which was part of their game, and whispered, "Don't be bashful, Jackie. Tell me."

"You know."

"What do I know?"

"What I want."

"To tie me up with the stockings?"

Hazzard had nodded his assent bashfully, his hand still playing.

"Isn't there something else, darling?"

"Yes."

"What?"

"You know," he had whispered, his submission arousing to him—and to her, he had presumed.

"You have to tell me. That's the game."

"I can't."

"Do you want me to walk for you?" she had asked, feigning impatience.

"M-hm."

"With my hands tied?"

"If you want to."

But then, of course, she had dashed his expectations, as the rules of their game required.

"I'm starving," she had announced imperiously, suddenly standing. "Let's eat."

"Where?" he had said.

"You decide, darling. You're the man."

"I thought maybe the Indian restaurant."

"Oh, I don't feel like Indian food tonight."

"Chinese?"

"I want Italian. But not at that place round the corner."

She had positioned herself directly before him, standing superciliously with her hands on her hips.

After careful consideration, Hazzard had answered, "I know a nice place on the East Side I think you'll like."

They had paused then to touch glasses and drink, Hazzard remembered now, stroking more swiftly in the shower.

"Do you like the way I look tonight?" she had asked then, still standing above him, her legs splayed, the skirt, therefore, quite high on her thighs.

"I always like the way you look."

"Yes? And do you love me?"

"Insanely."

"Do you want to make love with me right now?" She had referred to his crotch before meeting his eyes again; and in response, Hazzard had expressed his desire by reaching his hand beneath the skirt.

"Then say it," she had said.

"Say what?"

" 'I love you insanely.' "

"I love you insanely."

"Marcelline."

Hazzard had stood and pressed himself against her.

"I love you insanely, Marcelline."

"Did you miss me this week?"

"What do you think?"

"I hate it," she had whispered, her mouth touching his, "when I'm so busy with my PR work that I can't see you and fuck together."

They had kissed then with hot open mouths tasting of vodka.

"Did you jerk off thinking of me, darling?"

"Not telling."

"Be fun. Tell."

"Once."

"Yes! What did you think about? What were we doing?"

"Tell you in the bedroom."

"Later. Because I've made reservations at an Italian restaurant in Brooklyn."

"Brooklyn?"

"You should be happy. Now you can play with me in the cab."

"You bitch," he had answered, biting her upper lip.

Smiling, Marcelline had said, "You know I know much better than you what keeps you loving me."

Spent now at dawn in December, Hazzard stepped from the shower and wrapped himself in his tattered terry-cloth robe. He wiped clear the mirror with his hand and, eying himself skeptically, covered his face with shaving cream to keep the stainless-steel blade from nicking his throat.

When they'd returned much later that Halloween night from the restaurant in Brooklyn and he'd unbuttoned her blouse in the bedroom, Marcelline had announced that she would be leaving the next day for Rome, where she'd appear in court to resolve the requisite custody procedures for her son, for whom she wanted visiting privileges during his Christmas and summer vacations. After the proceedings, she had added casually, she would "jet" to Gstaad with "a friend" for a two-week skiing vacation.

"This friend, I presume," Hazzard had said, his hands

stroking her breasts beneath her blouse, "is a man?"

"Of course. What do you think I am, a lesbian?"

"I wouldn't consider such unnatural acts beyond you."

"Really, Jack," she had said impatiently, "don't be stupid. I'm not married to you."

He had tried to remain calm, but his hands, moving upward from her breasts to her throat, revealed his wrath.

"What the hell has marriage got to do with it?"

"Everything, darling. Because I'm free now to do what I want, whenever I want to. And my freedom is more important to me than any man."

Closing his eyes, Hazzard had removed his hands from beneath the beige blouse.

"If you don't mind," he had told her then, "I'm going to insist that you leave."

"Oh, really! We're only lovers, darling."

"I'm tired of just being lovers."

"Just what is it you want from me? Do you want to marry me?"

"That would only accelerate the abuse, don't you think?"

"I think," she had said emphatically, "that I don't have to explain myself to you. Because explanations bore me, and I hate to be bored."

"Then take your boredom and get out."

She had lit a cigarette.

"Listen, darling. You are free to threaten me or make love to me. Which one of them do you want?"

"Get lost," he had told her, interlacing his fingers before bending them backward to crack the knuckles.

"I don't understand what that means."

"It means 'Ciao.' "

She had wheeled abruptly from him, her heels clacking down the hallway to the door.

"Don't miss me too much, Charlie," she had said before slamming the door so swiftly that the bell chime reverberated long after the sound of her shoes had disappeared down the stairwell.

And now, eight weeks later, she had left a message on Hazzard's answering machine to say how much she wanted to fuck with him.

Three

HAZZARD stood in his bathrobe in the kitchen pondering nothing more profound than the percolating coffee. Outside, snow fell steadily from the dawn sky onto the silent city; and just as dreamily, Hazzard wondered what to do about the phone message.

"Of course he wonders what to do," the Father in him chastised, "because he doesn't listen to me anymore!" "It's not my fault," said the Son obsequiously, "it's the Lover's." And as the frightened Boy appealed to the Mother, the Father said caustically to the Lover, "I didn't think you were even attracted to girls." "You're the one who hates women," the Paranoid replied to the Father. "Not women," the Father amended mordantly, "only your mother!" "Just get on the horn and call the bitch," the Punk said resolutely.

Hazzard extinguished the blue flame beneath the pot and absently reached for a coffee mug.

"I knew this would happen," said the Recluse. "I warned everyone last spring not to call her." "But I was lonely," said the Boy. "That's right," affirmed the Lover, "I phoned out of loneliness." "One look at those legs of hers," said the Punk, "and I couldn't resist. I wanted a poke at her real bad." "I knew it was you!" said the Paranoid. "You and that priapic cock of yours!" And turning to the others in Hazzard's Head, the Paranoid warned, "And don't think this Punk won't call her again!"

Hazzard watched the snow settling slowly over the accumulating commuter traffic before pouring the coffee and moving to the living room. Sitting on the sofa, he stared at the phone on the end table.

From the very first the Lover in Hazzard had been smitten with Marcelline Tatia. That fateful November day, fourteen months ago now, she had been wearing a white cotton skirt, white stockings and red high heels. "There was a tear in the right stocking," recalled the Punk, "that went all the way up her thigh." "She was beautiful," said the Lover. "Just like Mommy!" added the Boy.

Marcelline Tatia had dropped a grocery bag onto the sidewalk and the Actor in Hazzard had knelt beside her to offer assistance. "Beaver shot par excellence," the Punk recollected.

"I'll get you another bag," Hazzard had volunteered.

"It's not necessary, thank you."

"No, no, it's my pleasure," the Lover had insisted, Hazzard disappearing into the grocery for a simple brown bag (into which he would toss the next year of his life).

"If we'd only minded our business," mused the Recluse. "But my life had no meaning," rejoined the Depressive. "I had nothing to lose." "Oh," said the Paranoid, "there's always something to lose."

Repacking the grocery items for her, Hazzard had requested the privilege of carrying the bag to her residence.

Marcelline Tatia had assented. "I'm just around this next corner."

"My name's Jack Hazzard."

She told him hers with a bashful aversion of her eyes that immediately endeared her to the Lover.

Notwithstanding the Actor's beguiling postures, the Son's sexual shame left the Lover stilted and shy, an affectation, the Patient inferred, serving to compensate for the Punk's eroticized hostility. The Recluse, consequently, conscious of a vicious conflict in Hazzard's libidinal life, opted for seclusion: He knew that what some of Hazzard desired, others could not love; and what some of Hazzard loved, others could not desire. Still, the Actor was undaunted: Hazzard's life was a game to him; he was dedicated to dramatic fun and games, no matter how inauthentic. Acting, the Actor appropriately assumed, was quite simply the only way Hazzard could enjoy himself. Indeed, as the Boy had recited over and over in Hazzard's youth, so now the Actor declaimed histrionically in Hazzard's Head in his adulthood: "I'm only playing!"

Hazzard sipped the coffee and smoked a cigarette.

"Banged her the next night," mused the Punk. "Did it never occur to you," interposed the humorless Patient, "that she banged you, as it were?" "That's right," said the Paranoid, sighing with relief. "She made me fuck her brains out!" "She said I was shy," said the Lover. "She took my hand and we went into the bedroom," added the Boy. "Bitch came all night, man," said the Punk. "I'd get her going and she'd finish herself off with her finger." "Symbolically castrating us," said the Patient. "But that's what women do," the Son said, turning to the Father, who nodded and thrust his hands lamely into his pockets. "Take your hands out of your pockets!" reproved the Mother, the Punk mumbling, "Pocket pool!"

Stimulating her clitoris with three fingers of her right hand while Hazzard ate her that first night together, she came in his mouth, moaning and writhing, her painted fingernails clacking against Hazzard's teeth, his tongue tasting and taking her as she languorously came. Thereafter, he took her from behind. "I dogged her all right," boasted the Punk. "Boom bam bang! Pumped her good!"

Taking her that way, from the blind side, as the Punk thought of it, Hazzard watched Marcelline's hands gripping the sheets before her as she collapsed breathlessly onto her stomach. Still inside her, Hazzard continued moving, more slowly, as slowly as her breathing, until he came in a lashing explosion of release. Later, his head buried in her long auburn hair, the Lover massaged and kissed her shoulders before the Punk and the Boy in Hazzard slid teasingly down, kissing and licking before reaming her.

"I love so much the way you fuck me, darling," she had said huskily. "I love the way you lick my ass and cunt." And later, supine beneath Hazzard, she'd looped her arms round his neck and whispered, "I love your nose and eyes, darling. I love the way you fuck me."

"I'm nothing without her," conceded the Depressive now as Jack Hazzard lit a second Lucky and, staring at the telephone through the coffee's curling steam, debated within himself whether or not to respond to Marcelline's message of the previous evening.

Drugs had been employed to embellish their lovemaking: cocaine, Quaaludes, wine, hashish, amyl nitrate.

"I saw into her soul," lyricized the Lover, the look of her lambent eyes lodged indelibly in his part of Hazzard's memory. "You mean her hole," said the Punk. "I cried in her arms," admitted the Depressive, the disconcerted Boy confessing, "I thought I was holding on to Mommy!" "I thought Marcelline was Love at last," conceded the Actor to the Lover. "What a night," resumed the Punk, winking to the Son as the Father eavesdropped. "I got reamed, steamed and dry-cleaned!" "I've never heard such vile language!" the Mother cried, withdrawing a bar of soap in Hazzard's Head with which to wash out the Boy's "filthy dirty" mouth. "At least he's attracted to girls," said the Father, squeezing the Son around the neck in a gesture of ambiguous intention while whispering conspiratorially, "For a long time back there I thought you might become a fagala. You know, those tight pants and that long hair!"

Dreamily, Hazzard turned his attention from the telephone and opened a book the Patient had recently acquired for the edification of the Writer; and so within the dim suffusion of winter light filtering through the dusty windows of the living room, Hazzard read:

> The basic condition for neurotic love lies in the fact that one or both of the "lovers" have remained attached to the figure of a parent, and transfer the feelings, expectations and fears one once had toward father or mother to the loved person in adult life; the persons involved have never emerged from a pattern of infantile relatedness, and seek for this pattern in their affective demands in adult life. In these cases, the person has remained, affectively, a child of two, or of five, or of twelve, while intellectually and socially he is on the level of his chronological age. . . . There are many individualized forms of the pathology of love, which result in conscious suffering and which are considered neurotic by psychiatrists and an increasing number of laymen alike. Some of the more frequent ones are briefly described in the following examples.

Four

THE resolution of the Patient as he closed the book for Hazzard left the Lover undeterred; he turned his attention to the telephone as the Punk drew deeply on his Lucky Strike. "Bingo!" boomed the Punk, sensing Hazzard's self-destructive impulse to phone. "Don't!" entreated the Patient, the Writer carping, "I've got a difficult scene to write this morning; I can't fuck around with the Lover's addiction!" "Fuck the scene!" cried the exuberant Punk as the Lover announced conclusively, "I'm calling her back." "Masochist," grumbled the Patient, staring at the Son in Hazzard's Head.

Hazzard lifted the receiver and dialed Marcelline's number from memory. Outside the window, two pigeons sailed swiftly down and away, snow swirling in big wet flakes in their wake.

"Hello?"

"Marcelline?"

"Yes?"

From the timbre of her perplexed and raspy voice, Hazzard inferred he had awakened her.

"It's Jack."

He heard the sound of sheets ruffling and the sigh of a match flaring, and he imagined her sitting up in bed.

"How are you, my darling?"

"Not bad. You?"

"I miss you."

"I miss you, too," he said.

"Good," she said, yawning, "because I only slept with someone sometimes to try to forget you. And you?"

"I?" Hazzard said sardonically. "I suppose I should be glad that you didn't forget about me."

"That's right, darling. Because I love you more than ever. Did you call me back because you miss making love with me?"

"Yes."

"I miss making love with you so much!"

"I want to see you, Marcelline."

"I want to see you too, Jackie."

"When?"

"Tonight?"

"Good."

There was a silence now in which Hazzard listened to her exhaling smoke.

"I hate it so much when we fight," she said.

"So do I."

"How's your novel coming?"

"I put it aside because of that screenplay deal."

"I'd love you even more if you were rich."

"I bet."

"That's why you mustn't take my not seeing you a lot so personally. Since you're not rich yet I have to work very very hard at my Public Relations."

"We can talk about that tonight," Hazzard said, the Writer impatient now to commence work, the flamboyant Actor bored by the Lover's caution.

"I don't want to talk with you tonight, darling. I want to make love with you and hold you. Are you still seeing that stupid psychiatrist?"

"Yes."

"What's he say?"

"About what?"

"About us, darling. Did you tell him you broke up with me?"

"Of course I told him."

"What did he say?"

"That I shouldn't see you again."

"Yes!" Amusement signaled in her voice. "And what did you say?"

"Does it matter?"

Marcelline laughed now. "I love it so much that you spend money to talk about me. You're so bizarre, Jackie."

"How's eight o'clock?"

"Will you make dinner for me? Because I love your chili."

"Why not?" Hazzard said, but the Punk was not at all happy with the Lover's accommodation.

"Do you still have some Quaalude?"

"Naturally,"

A clicking sounded on the line.

"There's my other phone, darling. See you around eight. I love you. Ciao."

Hazzard listened to the hang up tone rankle in his head as the relief the Lover in him had anticipated failed to register. Instead, the Paranoid's anxiety began to percolate wildly. "Now you've done it!" he rebuked the Punk, telling the Recluse, "Go on! Tell the Punk how you feel now. How we'll never get any peace with that bitch around." "You want peace of mind," the Punk told the Recluse, "but I want piece of ass. You lose, sucker!" "Up yours!" said the Mother, resentful that she would have to market and cook supper for the Lover's "tramp" of a girlfriend. "I'm sorry," said the infantilized Son, holding to the Father for security from Hazzard's Head as the Boy ran to the Mother with coincident alarm. "God knows I don't want to do this to us," announced the Depressive, "but you bastards leave me no choice." "No!" screamed the Boy. "Don't make us depressed! What'd I do bad, what'd I do bad?" "It's a long, unpleasant story," sighed the Patient, who said, turning to the Writer, "Perhaps you'd be kind enough to help me explain it to them?" "I'm afraid I haven't decent time," said the Writer vaingloriously. "I've a screenplay to write to pay the bills around here."

Five

S INCE the Writer in Hazzard's Head related to Jack Hazzard merely as a means to his dubious literary ends, he morbidly depended upon and relished Hazzard's psychic turmoil: his anxiety, obsessiveness, grandiosity, rage and depression. For if there were a story in happiness, then one would certainly never find the unhappy Writer interested in composing it: the subject, quite simply, was too alien to him. The Writer, therefore, was invested in contributing to Hazzard's unhappiness. Unfortunately for him, there were now so many unhappy inhabitants in Hazzard's Head that the Writer frequently found Jack Hazzard too debilitated by depression to wake and write. To wit, though the Writer depended on Hazzard's conflicts and ambivalences to fuel his imagination, frequently (especially circa his obsession with Marcelline Tatia) his neurosis ushered the Writer into a labyrinth of paralyzing contradictions. Consequently, the Writer became as despondent and insecure as the Depressive, indulging himself in doubts about the worth of his arduous and unremunerative existence. Indeed, it got so bad that the Writer came to empathize (even identify) with the Depressive's sense of impoverishment, the Recluse's requirement for isolation, the rage of the arrested Punk and the grasping, passive fantasies of salvation of the Lover. The Writer even understood why the Patient had enlisted the services of a psychiatrist. In fact, at such times when Hazzard's conflicts paralyzed him, the Writer remained frozen before the typewriter, fearing for his preeminent status in Hazzard's Head.

Thus the Writer condescended to continuously cajole the others, especially the Depressive. "Depression," he would tell the Depressive, "is a privileged mode of perception. I'm nothing without your unceasing self-inflicted sorrows. You're the very source of my creativity. You're a genius!"

Most of the time the Writer's shamelessly grandiose wheedling worked, with the desperate Depressive as well as with the others. For example, the Writer would explain to the Mother and the Father that though he, too, disapproved of the behavior of the amoral Actor, he, the Writer, would become dramatically impotent without the Actor's uncanny capacity to suspend disbelief and enter the more askew worlds of various characters whom he helped the Writer imagine. Moreover, without the autoerotic Boy, the Writer might not be so capable of compulsively playing alone with words with such dutiful effervescence. As for the Recluse, he inured Hazzard to the joyless solitude of the writing vocation, for the Recluse could remain alone in Hazzard's apartment for days and weeks and months, happily isolated from what the Father in Hazzard's Head so-called "the real world." Even the incorrigible Punk, recognizing how attracted women were to Hazzard's status as "Writer," encouraged the scribbler to compose another book so that he might recruit "a new infield" of admiring and adoring lovers. And, of course, the Lover naively savored the glamour of writing, fantasizing romantically that Hazzard might one day be remembered with all the solemn reverence reserved for such psychologically deformed literary predecessors as Lord Byron or Franz Kafka. As for the Paranoid, the Writer employed his neurotic reflex to externalize the fears and wishes of Hazzard's own psychic economy, thereby allowing the Writer to write about characters interpersonally conflicted in just such a way as he, Hazzard, was privately conflicted.

Sure, the Writer used Hazzard. But had he not, Hazzard would have gone broke! Dramatizing neurosis, no matter how banal its nature, was the Writer's only known way of assuring Hazzard financial solvency. Of course, on the upside, thanks to the distracting nature of the Writer's imaginary preoccupations, Hazzard negotiated an uneasy psychological alliance by distracting himself from himselves. In fact, a majority of Hazzard seemed most proud of the creative productivity of their neurotic character—at least until Hazzard's sexual obsession with Marcelline Tatia mobilized and gave focus to everything ungovernably contradictory in Hazzard's Head. And though the Writer increasingly feared the imminence of a nervous breakdown, he comforted himself with the idea that no matter what happened to Hazzard short of suicide, he, the Writer, would undoubtedly live to write a book about it.

"You are one sick soul," the Patient concluded anxiously, knowing a rationalization when he found himself living one.

Six

I N the beginning, of course, there had not been thirteen inhabitants of Hazzard's Head. Initially, in fact, Jack Hazzard had been simply Baby Jackie, to whom and for whom his mother was everything, the only thing. Actually, according to the Patient, the Boy adored his mother. She fulfilled his needs: gave him her tit, wiped his ass, dried him when he was wet and warmed him when he was cold; in short, his mother replaced the Boy's pain with pleasure, and taught him how to confuse the two. The Boy was helpless without his mother. He could not conceive of himself without first reacting to the requirements of his mother. The Boy was his mother; he was she, the Mother.

"Quite a story you've got here," the Writer remarked skeptically to the Patient one lonely afternoon following a dreary morning of writing about Hazzard's Head. But the Patient was more than a little contentious on the subject. "It's not a story," he replied in such a distemperate tone of condescension that the Writer elected not to pursue the matter

further. But the Patient persisted, nonetheless. "Story!" he
scoffed. "Science isn't a story. And furthermore, it's not my
story, but rather Doctor Freud's *science*. I assume you can
appreciate the methodological differences between psychoanalysis and storytelling?"

Frankly, the quarrelsome propensities of the Patient did
little, if anything, to dissuade the Writer's doubts about the
psychoanalytic story of the human psyche, especially since he
first inhabited Hazzard's Head some twenty-two years after
the birth of Baby Jackie and was dependent, therefore, on
the neurotic points of view of the Boy, Son, Mother, Father,
Depressive, Punk, Paranoid, Recluse, et al., in understanding the Lover's so-called obsession with Marcelline Tatia.

In any event, according to the Patient, rather too rapidly
for the Boy, Hazzard's Head housed a quartet of inhabitants
with very different needs and roles. "Quartet," insists the
Patient, for naturally, when Baby Jackie the Boy became
conscious of his father, he concurrently learned of the existence of the Son. Nevertheless the Boy cleaved obstinately
and exclusively to his mother, who didn't get along with his
father. The Boy created the Son to *care for* the Father.

Though his father was not supportive of the Son in the way
his mother was protective of the Boy, the Son nevertheless
worshipped his father, who was tall, hirsute and muscular (at
least to the Son, who could not conceive of himself without
fulfilling the commands of his father). The Son was his father;
he was he, the Father.

Hazzard, therefore, was they; or conversely, they were he,
Jack Hazzard, all four of him already in his head when he was
only two years old.

But the Son and the Boy were different inhabitants, just as
his father and mother were different parents. The Boy was
afraid of the more aggressive Son and ran to the Mother in

Hazzard's Head for protection. For example, when his father placed Jack Hazzard on a bicycle and encouraged him to *ride away!* the Boy within would commence to cry. As his father ran dutifully up and down the street alongside the bicycle, supporting the seat beneath Jack Hazzard and shouting encouragement, the Boy (despite the Son's valiant efforts to please the Father in Hazzard's Head) wanted only to be in the kitchen with his mother. "Sissy!" snapped the Son to the Boy, as Jack Hazzard fell from the bicycle, crying, "Mommy!" and ran into the house so his mother could kiss the booboo on his hand and *there now* make it all better.

His father taught Jack how to throw and catch a ball, but the ball scared the Boy. His father bought a tent for the yard, but the tent was cold and dark inside and the Boy was afraid to enter it even when the Son wanted to. "Fag!" the Son told the Boy inside Hazzard's Head, with the hope that the Father in him would be proud of the way the Son disparaged the apprehension of the Boy, whose behavior was informed by a desire to earn the approbation of his mother.

"What's he crying about now?" asked his father.

"Jackie," said his mother, "what's wrong, dear?"

"Nothing," said the Boy, thumb in his mouth as he clutched his mother's skirt and hid his head between her legs.

The Boy had learned to be afraid from his mother, who was afraid of everything, especially afraid of Jack's father, not to mention of herself and her own mother and father. The Son hated the Boy for being afraid like his mother, for his father (whom the Son idolized and idealized) disparaged fear. "Can't live in fear, son," his father insisted each time he discovered Jack sitting mutely in his room instead of playing with the neighborhood children, of whom the Boy in Jack was afraid. "Mommy said it was okay," the Boy answered as the Son in his head mimicked the whiny Boy:

"Mommy's afraid and so am I! I'm a little sissy! A little faggy fool!"

In no time Hazzard was as afraid of the judgments he passed on himself as he was of the judgments his parents levied on him. In other words, Hazzard was as afraid of himself as the Boy was afraid of the Son, as the Son was afraid of the Father, as the Father was afraid of the Mother, and as the Mother was afraid of the Father: as without, so within.

To abate his anxiety and insecurity, Jackie cleaved to his mother; he hid timidly by her side in the kitchen. Her dress was warm like the stove next to which she stood preparing Daddy's and Jackie's nice dinner. Jackie's mouth was warm, too. Whenever he stuck his thumb in his mouth he felt warm all over rather than cold all over. The Boy sucked Hazzard's thumb until he was ten; sucking his thumb made him feel less afraid of himself.

If the Boy had Hazzard suck his thumb for security, the Son had Hazzard suck up to his father for security. Indeed, the Son aligned Hazzard to his father with a passionate in-gratiation commensurate with the Boy's morbid grasping to his mother. At the same time, the Son wanted to be as strong and independent as he imagined (inaccurately) his father to be. (In truth, his father was feckless and narcissistically crippled.) But the Boy was afraid the Mother wouldn't love (approve of) him if the Son became as self-absorbed and detached as his father (now the Father also); and so the external conflicts brought forth internal tyrannies of ever-increasing convolutions.

Though Hazzard sensed quite early on that his parents didn't love each other, the Boy in him wanted his mother to love him (Jack) at least; therefore, Hazzard had to choose between either the Boy and Mother or the Son and Father in his head. The Boy chose the Mother to please his mother.

The Son, alternatively, chose his father over the Boy and Mother in the hope of appeasing the Father. Consequently, when his father endeavored to show Jack that there was nothing to be afraid of, such as stepping into a pitched hardball, the Son found himself struggling to combat the nature of the Boy in himself; and when his mother encouraged Jackie to be gentle and devoted to her, the Boy found himself fighting against the Son in himself.

Now the more the insecure Boy was afraid (of himself and the world), the more desperately he cleaved to his mother. The enraged Son compensated by acting mean and bossy with his friends (of whom the Boy was afraid). The Son wanted his father to teach the Boy in his head how to be courageous and manly; but if his father was not present, then the Son in Jack Hazzard would stay with the Boy in the house near his mother. Although this behavior allayed the anxiety of the Boy, it infuriated the Son; and thus little Jack Hazzard discovered himself bored and temperamental. Where was his father, for Christ's sake! Why was he always away at the stupid shoe store? Because without his father the Son would be compelled to stay in the house with the scaredy-cat Boy, who was like a little girl!

The Son soon hated the Boy (himself) just as he imagined his father would want him to hate the Boy for living in fear. Increasingly Jackie brooded silently in his room, only to later display fits of temper in the presence of his parents.

The Patient deduces that Jack was four years old that April afternoon when his father brought home a puppy to keep his son company.

"Thanks, Dad. Thanks!"

But his mother didn't like the dog, Mike. Mike shed.

"Get that dog off your bed! Put that dog in the basement!"

"Sorry, Mom. Sorry."

It was during the summer of Jack's fourth year that the Depressive appeared in Hazzard's head to resolve as best he could the contradictions between the Son and the Boy.

"What'd you do today?" asked his father, when Jack was four. The Son wore a baseball cap as the Boy played with a monkey puppet on his right hand, Jack sitting at the kitchen table helping Mommy bake cookies.

"Jackie painted a tree with watercolors and helped me plant flowers," his mother answered, putting her arm around Jackie, who was now the "monkey-in-the-middle" of his parents' frustration with each other (which Jack was now recapitulating in his head).

"It was fun," said the Boy, nervously sidling up to his mother, whom the Son hated, as he could not be himself with her.

"Take your thumb out of your mouth," scolded his father.

Ashamedly withdrawing his thumb, the Son said, "I wanted to play ball but no one was around."

"That's because they're all in day camp," said his father.

"Jackie doesn't want to go to day camp," said his mother. "Don't make him feel guilty."

"*He* doesn't?" said his father, "Or *you* don't want him to?"

"Tell Daddy, Jackie," said his mother emphatically.

"I don't know," Jack said weakly, his eyes lowered, teeth tearing at his lower lip.

"Look at me, Jack," said his father, taking his son by the chin. "Do you want to go to day camp like all the other boys your age around here or do you want to stay home with your mother?"

"Tell Daddy what you told Mommy, Jackie. Go on. Don't be afraid. Just be honest, honey."

"Jack! God damn it, Jack, get back here! Now what's he crying about?"

"Jackie!" called his mother.

But Jackie had raced away to his room to stand sullenly before the closed window and stare mutely at his friends playing catch in the street. "Hey," said the Son, "let's go outside and play catch." "We'll hurt Mommy's feelings," said the Boy, preferring to hurt the Son's (his own). And for the first time in Hazzard's Head (that the Patient can remember, according to the Writer), the Depressive spoke to the other inhabitants. "Let's just stay in here and feel sad." "What the heck for?" protested the Son. "Isn't it preferable," answered the Depressive, "to making the Boy feel guilty every time you do something the Mother doesn't approve of, or of getting you angry every time the Boy acts like what the Father thinks makes you a wimp?"

But the Boy was terrified of the Depressive. "Don't make me sad!" the Boy screamed. "Don't make me hurt myself!"

"What's he crying about in his room now?" said his father, home at last from the shoe store.

"I don't know anymore," said his mother, who'd been in bed all day with a migraine headache.

"Son?" said his father, knocking on Jack's door and stepping cautiously into Jack's room. "What'd you do today, Jack?"

"Nothing."

"Is something wrong?"

"I don't know."

"You want to play catch?"

"No."

"What are you doing in your room? It's nice out."

"Nothing."

"You want to talk about it?"

"No."

. . .

When he was eight, Jack knocked on the door of his father's study and stepped cautiously inside.

"What is it, Jack?"

"What's guilt, Dad?"

"Guilt?" said his father, lowering the sail of newsprint. "I'd say guilt is what you try to make somebody feel to get them to do things your way."

"Do you ever try to make me feel guilty?"

"Only if you won't do things my way."

"I'd never want to make you feel guilty, Dad."

"A little guilt never hurt, remember that."

Sometime during Hazzard's eighth year, and for a long and not very nice time thereafter, something happened to the inhabitants of Hazzard's Head: the Depressive began to make them feel guilty for not doing things *their* way.

"Jackie," his mother said, "would you like to help Mommy make cookies?"

"I don't know," Jackie said, hearing Daddy's car pull in the driveway, his father home from the shoe store at last.

"Don't you like baking cookies with me anymore?"

"Daddy says only sissies bake cookies."

"When did Daddy say that?"

"I don't know—" hearing Daddy opening the front door.

"Where are you going, honey?"

Jackie went reflexively to his room and locked the door.

"Jesus Christ! Where's my newspaper?" Jack could hear Daddy hollering downstairs in the den.

"I made a hat for Jackie with it."

Daddy sounded mad coming up the stairs and knocking on the door, behind which Jackie hid with his thumb in his mouth.

"Jack? Is the paper in your room, son? Jack, open the door for your dad."

"No!"

Now with the door to his room locked, Hazzard discovered a new inhabitant in his head: the Recluse. "You won't hurt me, too, will you?" asked the Boy, Jack's thumb in his mouth as he eyed the locked door recalcitrantly. The Recluse winked at the Boy and said, "Keep the door locked and we'll be all right. Mind your business and keep away from the others, and I won't cause any trouble."

"Jack! I asked you if the newspaper is in your room. Did your mother make you a hat with my newspaper? Jack!"

"What?"

"I'll break down this door. Do you hear me?"

Jack Hazzard fearfully slipped the newspaper under his door and listened to his father gather up the pages.

"No dinner for you tonight, Jack. You just stay in that room until I say you can come out."

"Okay."

Seven

THE Son was more percipient than the Boy. Growing up, the Son observed things for Jack Hazzard about his mother and father that the Boy could not understand.

"Listen," said the Son, "they're fighting again." The Boy didn't want Jack Hazzard to listen at the top of the stairs; it scared him too much to listen. For his mother screamed hysterically at his father after Jackie had gone to bed. "Downstairs," said the Son in Hazzard's Head. "They're yelling again. They want a divorce. Listen." "Quit spying," whined the Boy. "Quit spying on Mommy and Daddy or else I'll tell the Depressive to get you!" "Go on!" hollered the Punk hatefully, appearing now for the first time in Hazzard's Head, as Jack Hazzard, age nine, began pacing in his bedroom, all mad and scared, unable to sleep, the Punk in him fed up with the Depressive and the Boy blaming the Son for what wasn't his fault!

At nine years old, Hazzard was *sent away,* unannounced, to a boy's summer camp in Maine. The Boy in him was terrified without his mother, the kitchen, the family house and the dog. Therefore the Punk emerged in Hazzard's Head in order to protect the Son from disclosing his fear to the Father in his head.

On the softball field that July, the Punk impelled Hazzard to tyrannize his adolescent companions. Running into right field, Hazzard, the bossy shortstop now, screamed at the outfielder, "Can't you catch? What are you, scared of a stupid little ball?" as the members of the opposing team hugged one another in the exuberance of victory.

"You suck!" the Punk required Hazzard to rage. "You made us lose!"

And Jack Hazzard pushed his teammate to the grass and kicked him. "Sissy!" the Son insisted Hazzard say. "Asshole!" the Punk had Hazzard holler. "Leave him alone!" the Boy and the Mother in Hazzard's Head cried, stunned and frightened by his own behavior.

The other boys on the team circled around Hazzard, and the outfielder's friend said, "Go on, Hazzard. Push *me* down."

"I'll kill you!" the Punk exploded, and Jack lunged viciously at the challenger. Hazzard was small, but the Punk in him was swift and mean; he crushed the challenger's head in his famous headlock, the Father commanding the Son, "Harder, man. Harder!" as the Boy screamed, "Stop it! You're hurting him!" the Punk chanting, "Kill, kill, kill!" as Hazzard crunched the kid's head as hard as he could.

"Give?" Hazzard grunted. "You give?"

"I give," whimpered his vanquished opponent.

When Hazzard released his teammate's head, he could see

at once that the boy's forehead was bruised, so that the Boy in Hazzard's Head (who identified with the weak and hurt) commenced to cry. To his surprise, Hazzard found himself penitently offering his opponent his hand.

"No hard feelings," the Father commanded Hazzard to say. "Good fight."

And though his opponent shook Hazzard's hand, the remorseful Boy and Mother aligned themselves with the Depressive; and suddenly Jack Hazzard felt isolated, afraid and angry at everyone. The Paranoid gazed apprehensively through Hazzard's eyes at the wall of boys encircling Jack. "You'd better watch yourself, chump!" he told the Son. "Who the hell are you?" said the Punk. "The product of your repressed rage and the Son's externalized hostility," responded the Paranoid icily.

Inhabiting Hazzard's Head for defensive purposes, the Paranoid forged a most destructive alliance with the Boy, legitimizing the Boy's infantile fears by projecting fearsome qualities onto other people and events, for the Son and the Father could not abide believing that Jack Hazzard possessed fears; no, it must be the world itself, or others, wherein danger and cowardice resided.

Thus the diffident Recluse found it ever so easy to convince the inhabitants of Hazzard's Head that a wise soul eschewed the snares and nets of the paradoxically cruel world. Thus the Boy used the Recluse to rationalize Hazzard remaining in his room (where he sequestered himself more and more as he grew older and older) to avoid conflicts between the Mother and the Father in his head, but which, paradoxically, ineluctably generated conflicts between the Boy and the Son in his head—conflicts which only the sadomasochistic Depressive was capable of resolving.

By the time he was ten, there were eight of Hazzard warring with himself. Perpetually anxious, he became increasingly shy and reclusive. The Punk, however, grew angrier and angrier as the Son, Boy, Depressive, Recluse and Paranoid evinced greater and greater insecurity. Thus the Actor was created by the Father and Mother to protect Hazzard from the shamelessly low sense of self-esteem he frequently revealed.

"Don't let him act so ineffectual and awkward around people," the Mother told the Actor. "Yes," said the Father, "he embarrasses me." "I'm sorry," said the Depressive, full of shame and self-loathing for the Boy and Son, who more and more frequently came to depend on the Actor to hide from others (and himselves) Hazzard's inferiority and paralyzing ambivalence.

The Actor compensated for Hazzard's inferiority by acting grandiosely. His thinking became ever more illogical. "Great men suffer," the Actor told the Depressive and the Son, and they extrapolated speciously, "Great men suffer, we suffer, therefore we are great men!" "I know," replied the Recluse ingenuously; but he secluded Hazzard from others for fear their evaluations might debunk the Actor's sophistic nonsense.

The Punk, of course, was fully supportive of camouflaging the Boy's whining, dependent and groveling ways. After all, it was the Punk's savage temper that allowed the Actor to disguise the Son's sense of humiliating inadequacy by humiliating other boys through the physical intimidation of crushing their faces in headlocks. "I ain't no pussy," the Punk would tell the Father. "I'm a fucking hardass, dig?"

Appropriately, Hazzard's generalized hostility left him feeling increasingly vulnerable to reprisals. Therefore the Paranoid's prominence ascended coincident to the Punk's; they kept the fragmented Hazzard forever circumspect, convincing him that it was others who were hostile and usurious, not himself (the Son, Father, Depressive, Actor, et al.). Actually, psychologically speaking, the Paranoid's projections were strategically necessary: only by way of externalization could Hazzard abate the accelerating guilt of his self-persecution, which was, in turn, informed by the relentless malefaction of his self-hatred.

Hazzard's self-hatred intrigued the Writer; he sensed it to be the ineluctable product of the Son's and Boy's ancient antagonism.

"Listen," the Boy told the Writer, "I used to watch Mommy get dressed and put on her makeup." "That's right," said the Punk, beating his meat to a porno magazine, "the bitch sat there without. . . ." "I did not!" hollered the Son, imploring the Father to believe him. "Yes, you did, Jackie," said the Mother. "You watched me in my panties and bra as I put on my face. Then you used to pick out my dress and zip me up." "She's lying!" raged the Son to the Father. "She took so God damn long," recalled the Father, "that I went downstairs to watch TV and read the paper." "I liked to watch," confessed the Boy. "I once saw that Mommy didn't have a pee-pee!"

"Hey!" cried his father, when Jack was twelve, "what's going on up there? We're late. Hey, Jack! What's going on up there with you and your mother?"

"Nothing!" cried his son.

"Quick, honey," said his mother. "Zip me up." Calling, "I'm coming, I'm coming! One sec." Saying to Jackie, "How do I look, honey?"

"Nice, Mom."

"Beautiful?"

"Hey, Jack! What's your mother doing up there?"

"I'm coming, Irv! Do I look beautiful, honey?"

"Hurry up already, Mom!"

"Does my tushie look too big in this dress?" Craning her neck to see. Jack, nervous, yelling, "I don't know. Hurry up already, Mom!"

"Jack?"

"I'm coming, Irv, I'm coming. Honey, quick, put a hanky in my pocketbook."

"Where's your hanky?"

"In the drawer with my panties and falsies."

"Jack, what the hell is going on up there?"

"She's coming, she's coming!"

"Why do all your pajama bottoms have holes in the crotch?" his mother asked repeatedly from the time Hazzard was twelve until he left for college. "What do you do to yourself when your door's closed?"

The truth (the Paranoid swears) was that the bottoms either ripped from the wear of repeated washing and drying or from Hazzard's kicking them off late at night when the furnace made the room too warm.

"Nothing," answered her son laconically, Hazzard ashamed but not understanding really.

"I'll bet nothing!" the Mother answered now in Hazzard's Head, scrutinizing the Son with one eye closed and her head cocked suspiciously.

Eight

Now in December, after the Writer in Jack Hazzard surrendered to the exhaustion of an unsatisfying four hours struggle to write about the etiology of his character's self-hatred, he meditated listlessly in the kitchen on Hazzard's scheduled fiction reading the next evening at the New School. The Punk wanted him to read a pornographic selection from Hazzard's modest oeuvre, but the Actor preferred a piece that would evoke laughter. "Don't worry," the Punk quipped, "the Writer's pornography's a joke." Yet the Paranoid admonished the Writer against permitting the Actor to make a fool of Hazzard.

The Mother prepared Hazzard's sandwich grudgingly. She felt threatened by the Writer's and the Patient's dangerous dabbling in psychology; it gave the Boy ideas that challenged hers and the Father's punitive authority over Hazzard. Consequently, as Hazzard fumbled with lettuce and cheese and mayonnaise, the Mother commenced to complain that the apartment was freezing now at noon on this snowy December day and that Jackie might catch cold eating lunch in such a drafty place.

Hazzard found himself piling logs over crumpled newsprint in the fireplace and tossing in a match; and sitting nearby on the sofa the Recluse in Hazzard turned his attention from the warming flames to the Patient's ponderous psychology text.

"What about soup?" inquired the Boy, biting into the sandwich. But the Mother, in her displeasure with the Patient's snooping into their past, ignored the Boy.

"I assume the purpose of this reading is to further complicate things between me and Marcelline," complained the Lover. "It's about me!" said the Boy excitedly. "About why the Son and me became the Writer when we grew up."

> Artists of the detached type, who have demonstrated in their creative periods that they can not only feel deeply but also give expression to it, have often gone through periods, usually in adolescence, of either complete emotional numbness or of vigorous denial of all feeling. . . . The creative periods seem to occur when, following some disastrous attempt at close relationships, they have either deliberately or spontaneously adapted their lives to detachment . . . have become resigned to a kind of isolated living.

"Is that supposed to be news to me?" the Recluse asked the Writer.

> What all detached persons have in common . . . is their capacity to look at themselves with a kind of objective interest, as one would look at a work of art. . . . They may often, therefore, be excellent observers of the processes going on within them.

"It's true!" said the Boy, "I like playing with myself." "I dig playing with myself, too," said the Punk, whipping out his cock and stroking it until he climaxed.

The Artist who has withdrawn from reality into his fantasies, which represent derivatives of his Oedipus wishes and about which he feels guilty, finds his way back to the objective world by presenting it with his work. The acceptance of his work means for him that the public shares his guilt and this relieves him of his guilt feelings. The public, having Oedipus wishes of their own, admires the artist because he dares to express what they have repressed, and thus relieves them of their guilt feelings. . . .

"You're going to be late for your psychiatric appointment," the Mother said harshly, and Hazzard looked now at the clock on his writing desk. "Don't interrupt us," the Patient said calmly. But the Mother turned churlishly to the Boy. "You've got to scrub your teeth and dress. Hurry up!"

The conclusion we arrive at from these observations is that self-hate in all essentials is an unconscious process. In the last analysis there is a survival interest in not being aware of its impact. This is the ultimate reason that the bulk of the process is usually externalized, i.e., experienced as operating not within the individual himself but between him and the outside world. We can roughly distinguish between active and passive externalization of self-hate. The former is an attempt to direct self-hate outward, against life, fate, institutions, or people. In the latter the hate remains directed against the self but is perceived or experienced as coming from the outside. In both ways the tension of the inner conflict is released by being turned into an interpersonal one.

Hazzard closed the textbook.
"And don't forget to go to the bank," the Mother told the

Father in Hazzard's Head. "Because after Jackie's appointment I've got to go marketing for that little tramp the Lover loves."

Once dressed, overcoat and scarf in place, the Lover, Paranoid and Son in Hazzard popped a Valium in preparation for the Patient's session, which, the Mother and Father insisted, would only make things worse for Hazzard. "Of course the sessions are making things worse," said the Writer. "I'll be out of work if the damn Patient resolves our conflicts." "I'm leaving," the Patient told Hazzard; and he went out into the city.

The snow-filled park was beautiful to the Boy in Hazzard; he threw snowballs at trees and talked squeakily to the squirrels. The Depressive resisted and begrudged the Boy his ebullience; it only made him experience his melancholy more acutely. Meanwhile, the Father, in his resentment of Hazzard, had no patience with any of them. "We're late, damn it!" he said, scowling, Hazzard referring to his wristwatch and turning away from the Boy's fascination with the darting, playful squirrels. "His feet are all wet now," the Mother castigated, Hazzard shuffling slowly now in his Valium trance across the field on his way to the psychiatrist's Upper East Side office, the Patient wondering what to make of the never-ending voices, of which, he supposed, he was merely just one more.

Now with the aim of edifying, the Teacher spoke unto Hazzard. "Do not identify your true self with these voices," he said arcanely. "Not even with this voice. For your true self abides not in the mind." "Where then?" asked the Patient. "My dick?" guessed the Punk. "Consider," resumed the Teacher, *"that* which empowers the mind. Consider *that* animating energy which passes beyond understanding." "But that's epistemologically impossible," said the Writer.

The Teacher smiled and fell silent. "Oh, far out!" said the Paranoid cynically. "Another middle-class *mystic.*"

Hazzard traversed Fifth Avenue and climbed the winding front stoop of the brownstone to the black-gated glass door. Signaling his arrival on the intercom, he waited for the buzzer to sound; then he climbed five flights of stairs, hung up his coat and scarf in the closet in the doctor's waiting room, and sat.

He could hear Dr. Roth conversing on the telephone in muted tones beyond the closed door before him. Despite the Valium, Hazzard's apprehension registered palpably, and he smoked a cigarette while reading an article on mass starvation in the so-called Third World. The Depressive in him wondered why the periodical's editors weren't comparably concerned with the mass psychological starvation in the post-industrial continents? "Think real hard, dick brain," the Punk responded derisively. "I will," said the earnest Patient defensively.

Roth opened the door, and Hazzard, shaking his hand, entered the office. They sat facing each other on chairs upholstered in corduroy. Roth was a lanky, sanguine man whose penchant for tweed suits inspired Hazzard to conjecture mean-spiritedly why the man hadn't chosen advertising or gynecology as his vocation.

"Snowing," Hazzard began, glancing past Roth to the window of dreary winter light.

"I'm told."

Hazzard was in pain and wanted to weep; instead, he cleared his throat and cautiously lit a cigarette. "Don't say anything that will embarrass me," the Father warned the Son. "Got it covered, pops," the Actor replied.

"Marcelline called me last night," Hazzard began tentatively. "She left a message on my answering machine. I phoned her this morning."

Hazzard paused, the Son afraid of the Father, but the Boy cried, "I'm telling, I'm telling!" "Do that," encouraged the Patient.

"I've invited her for dinner tonight," Hazzard said.

Roth nodded.

"Don't you have anything to say?"

"I'd prefer to hear what you have to say," Roth said.

"I'm in pain," Hazzard answered. "I'm scared."

"That surprises you?"

"I thought I'd feel better if I contacted her."

"In what way?"

"I don't know exactly."

"Think about it."

Hazzard moved his eyes to the window.

"I've been anxious without her. I thought if I phoned I wouldn't feel anxious anymore."

"Yet the anxiety persists?"

The Paranoid rolled his eyes at the Patient in Hazzard's Head. "How much you paying this mountebank?" "Screw you," said the Writer, "it's my money the Patient's wasting."

"Anxiety's worse," Hazzard said.

"Are you afraid of Marcelline?"

"You know I am."

"Do you think fear motivated you to return her call?"

Hazzard took pause to consider. "I'm not sure I follow."

"Did you *want* to call her?"

"As opposed to what?"

"Feeling compelled."

Hazzard shrugged. "I thought it would alleviate my anxiety."

"What exactly have you been anxious about?"

"I'm lonely," Hazzard whispered. "And I don't know what to do about it anymore."

"Does Marcelline make you feel less lonely?"

Hazzard sent a plume of smoke to the ceiling and kept his eyes there. "I'm scared that if I don't see her she'll sleep with someone else."

"That's why you invited her for dinner?"

"It scares me to think about that."

"Her sleeping with someone else?"

"What the hell do you want me to say?" Hazzard exploded. "That I'm trying to keep myself from sleeping with someone else?"

"Whom would you sleep with?" Roth asked calmly.

"You're the doctor; you tell me."

"What's this rage at me all about?"

"It's about you fucking with my head."

Dr. Roth stared evenly at Hazzard, observing.

Hazzard sighed and extinguished his cigarette. "Please," he said softly, "I've asked you a hundred times not to stare at me like that."

Hazzard kept his eyes averted during the ensuing silence.

Eventually Roth said, "I wonder if you're tempted to phone, say, your dad when you're feeling pained like this."

Hazzard snickered ambiguously.

Roth persisted. "You haven't seen him in how long now? Ten months?"

"Eleven."

"But you make sure to speak with him?"

"From time to time."

"You used to speak with him all the time, didn't you?"

"I used to do lots of things."

Roth said patiently, "Tell me a little bit about you and your dad, Jack."

When he was thirteen and depressed again, Jack sat somberly before his father during a conference in the study where his father sequestered himself each evening to watch TV and take a nap.

"What's wrong with me, Dad?"

"Sexual frustration."

"What's that mean?"

"Well," his father answered, glancing from the TV, "sex is the strongest drive in the universe. Once you've gotten laid you'll understand what you're missing. That's why you're frustrated but don't understand it yet."

"Is sex what happens when you love a girl?"

"Sometimes. But it's better if you don't love them."

"How come?"

"Because short-term sex is better than long-term sex."

"Do you love Mom?"

"Sometimes."

"Did you ever love any other girl before Mom?"

"You want to know the truth? I don't think I've ever really been in love."

"I've been in love."

"You! With whom?"

"Mike and you and Mom."

"That's different."

"How come?"

"There's no sex involved."

"Is sex fun?"

"Sure."

"What do you do in sex?"

"Hey, come on now. Let me watch the news here, okay?"

"Sorry. Dad?"

"What, Jack."

"Nothing."

"Go on, ask."

"Do you love me and Mike?"

"When you're a good boy and Mike's a good dog I love you, yes."

"Do you think I'm a good boy?"

"Yes."

"Thanks, Dad! I love you, too. Bye. Thanks."

"Hey, bring me a beer, will you?"

"Sure. You want your slippers, too, and the paper?"

"You've already brought me the slippers and the paper."

"Oh! Sorry."

"Jack?"

"Yes."

"Calm dówn, please. I don't like when you get as excited as your mother."

"Dad?"

"What?"

"Do girls like sex, too?"

"Only if you're not married to them."

"How come girls get married then?"

"So they don't feel guilty about having sex with you."

"But you just said . . ."

"Hey, just hurry up with that beer."

"Dad, do you teach me about sex or does Mom?"

"Ask your mother. And let me know what she tells you."

"Your mother and I," his father told Jack when he was fifteen and accompanying his father to the hardware store, "have a sexual problem. You see, your mother was a virgin when we were married. On our wedding night I discovered that my penis was too big for her. It's taken a great deal of patience on my part. I've tried to teach her.

"I have a sexual problem with your mother," his father told Jack. "I'm impotent with your mother. Not with other women, darn it, but with your mom I am.

"My idea of a perfect Sunday," said his father to Jack, "is to play a good set of tennis and come home and have relations with your mother. If I could only get her to brush her teeth first!"

"When I was engaged to your mother," his father said, another time, "I used to drop her off at her house and go to Myrna's house and have relations with her. Your mother wasn't about to put out before our wedding night. And then, when she finally did, well, then I discovered that my p—"

"I had an affair once," his father said yet another time. "Your mother found out because like a jackass I admitted it. Of course, no one knows about my extracurricular life— except you, I mean."

"Then why are you telling me?"

"What's the matter now?" said his mother, emerging exhausted from the kitchen, carrying a tray of brownies and tea into the living room.

"He just started crying," said his father.

"Crying? But I spent all day in the kitchen baking him these brownies he loves to eat so he can complain his face is full of pimples."

"What do you mean 'all day'?" his father said. "It can't take more than an hour."

"With the marketing and the cooking and the cooling it takes all day!"

"So it takes all day!" his father hollered. "What do you want from me—a medal?"

"I'm sorry," Jack said, leaving the living room.

When Hazzard was nineteen and had returned from the
university during Easter recess his father said one Saturday,
"Mind if I ask you a question?"

"What?"

"Am I correct in assuming you're getting laid in college?"

"That's none of your business."

"Don't be so defensive, for God's sake."

"I've got more important things to do."

"Name one."

"Earning good grades so I can be somebody when I grow
up."

"You can't get good grades and get laid?"

"I don't want to talk about it."

"Tell me this then. Why's your hair so long? Because, no
offense, Shirley, but from the rear I can't tell whether you're
a girl or a boy."

"Tap me on the shoulder next time you're confused."

"Very funny. Just do me a favor and get your hair cut, will
you?"

"Jesus Christ!"

"Don't be so sensitive, for God's sake."

As Hazzard left for the barber appointment, his father
called, "Get a real haircut now. Not just the ends trimmed.
Because I always wanted a daughter, but not one with whisk-
ers and a pecker!"

"Fuck off for once, Dad."

"Hey! What is it with you and your mother? Can't take a
little teasing?"

The barber's name was Sal.

"Not too short, Sal."

"You like it long, right?"

"That's right."

"Long, sure, but not too long, right? Long is okay. But too long and the girls don't go for it. Know what I mean?"

Hazzard didn't, exactly. "Just not too short, Sal."

"Not too short, not too long. I'll make it just the length the girls like it. You're a nice-looking fella. Handsome like your dad. They all love your dad, you know that, right? Handsome man, your dad."

"I know."

"They must all love you, too, right? Real ladies' man, right?"

"I guess."

"You guess—that's a good one. You guess! You kids are too God damn lucky for your own good. You must be getting it all day long at the university, am I right?"

"I do okay."

"Okay! Listen to this guy. Okay! Hey, let me ask you personally now, Jackie . . ."

"Jack."

"*Jack.* Sorry, Jack. Let me ask you personally what you think of this friend of mine."

Sal the barber reached into a drawer beneath a ledge on which stood black combs soaking in bottles of turquoise-colored cleansing agent and showed Hazzard a number of Polaroid shots of women wearing lacy black brassieres and panties.

"Take a look at these girls, Jack. Take a good long look and tell Sallie which you like most—you know, which gives you the hots."

"I don't know."

"You don't know?"

"Hey, don't cut so much off."

"Don't know? A good-looking fella like yourself don't know? Come on. Just between me and you—which one?"

Hazzard pointed. "This one, I guess."

"Alice! You got taste just like your dad. Let me get her on the phone here. She loves guys with long hair."

"But you just cut all mine off."

"Long, Jack. But not too long. Here, let me just get her on the line." While dialing, Sal said, "Because I know she'll love you and you'll love . . . Hello? Alice? Hey, Sallie here. Listen, doll, I got a knockout of a kid in my chair who's a real college genius who wants to say hello. Okay, hold on just a sec."

Sal the barber handed Jack the phone.

"Go on. Give a middle-aged broad a thrill. She loves young guys with long hair. Go on now."

Confused and chagrined, Hazzard said cautiously, "Hello?"

"Hi there. I'm Alice. Sallie tells me you're real cute."

"I don't know."

"I bet you are. You like my picture?"

"Sure."

"Will you come visit me?"

"I don't even know you."

Sal said in Jack's ear, "Be nice to her, she's lonely."

"But I'd like for you to get to know me," Alice said. "Wouldn't you like that?"

"See, the thing is," Hazzard told her, "I go to school in Iowa. So I'm not around too much."

"Super. We'll party before you go back. Sallie will give you my number 'case you want to play. Okay, hon?"

"Okay," Hazzard acceded, thinking, *She must be desperate or something.* "But my hair's not long anymore."

"What?"

"Well, uh, Sal . . . Sallie said you like guys with long hair."

"You just come see me. We'll party. Gimme Sallie now, hon."

"Okay. So long. Thanks."

Sal took the phone, laughed once or twice, then hung up. Trimming Hazzard's sideburns, he said, "You go see Alice. She loves young guys. Your dad's taken care of everything."

"He paid for the haircut?"

"He's covered everything, kid."

As Hazzard left the barbershop, Sal handed him his card with Alice's phone number on the back.

"Remember," he told Hazzard, "Long, but not too long. Too long hurts, right?"

"Right," Hazzard said, pocketing the card, which he would later toss out the window while driving home.

Roth referred to his wristwatch. "I'm afraid we'll have to stop until tomorrow."

"I wonder why he set me up like that?"

"We'll resume tomorrow at two."

"What about tonight?"

"We'll talk about tonight tomorrow."

Hazzard stood hesitantly and shook Roth's hand. "Thanks."

"For what?"

Hazzard shrugged and exited the office. In the outer room another patient was waiting.

Nine

THE snow was falling faster now as Hazzard walked into the park, still ruminating about his relationship to his father.

"We can't preoccupy ourselves with your father right now," the Mother said. "I've got to shop for that little whore Jackie's going to see this evening." "I'm old enough to do my own marketing," said the Lover. "Let's not fight for once," the Son said, imploring the Father to silence the Mother. "The only way to turn off that hag is to cold-cock her with a right hook," said the Punk. "Or stick your tongue in her mouth!" cracked the Father. "Leave Mommy alone!" screamed the Boy.

The Teacher spoke now. "This consciousness of blame will not bring us the peace for which we long." "Who longs for peace?" the Writer replied, the Punk adding, "Don't call us, Mystery Man, we'll call you." "After you've put childish things behind you," the Teacher told the Boy, "perhaps then

I shall be of help." "You leave Jackie alone!" the Mother said. "Hey, kid," the Punk inquired of the Boy, "you ever eat pussy?" "Jesus Christ," the Depressive told the Lover, "I need a drink."

Thinking about a martini, the Patient remembered now what he had forgotten to show Roth. Hazzard reached into the pocket of his overcoat.

"Do you remember these letters?" the Patient asked the Writer, as Hazzard wandered down a snowy path and unfolded epistles composed to Hazzard's father when the Son, age nine, ruled in Hazzard's Head.

"Where did you get these?" the Father asked suspiciously. "Father sent them to me," the Patient said. "He'd kept them for some reason."

Hazzard brushed snow from a bench facing a frozen pond and sat down to read.

Dad
    Since you wouldn't let me talk I hope you read this. I don't care what momy thinks or anybody thinks. I know Im write. I know 9 OUT of 10 things I do are wrong. But still I do one thing write. Dad you got to Believe me because noBody Else does. especially MoMmy. Please don't give me a lesten on the words I spelled wrong.

                                                                Jack

"What's your point?" asked the Father. "I'm not certain," the Patient replied, frowning, the Son looking sullenly at the Father. "What's the difference?" the Depressive said. "The damage's been done." "That's right," concurred the Paranoid. "Start digging things up and the Son will only get worse." Nevertheless, the Patient persisted in his reading, snow sliding down the page of the next note.

Dear Dad and Mom,

I've been thinking and have come to the conclusion that I dont fit in the family. I guess Im the "reject" in our family. I never shovel the walk on time, Im fresh, greedy, a cry baby, a sore head, and kind of stupid. You see, Im pretty bad after all. The only thing Im good at is being nice to animals. Im not feeling sorry for my self either. Im just facing the facts really. And also another good thing about me is that I try, but things always turn out bad. The only thing that puzzles me is that I would appreciate knowing why you think I have so many privileges.

Your Rejected Son, Jack

Dad

You are all so worried about my social life with girls so I will tell you. Im not the most popular kid in 7th grade nor an average kid with girls. Im popular, girls like me and I like them. And No I don't have a girl friend yet.

Jack

Brushing snow from the shoulders of his overcoat, Hazzard stood now in the fading afternoon light and walked from the park.

"Big fucking deal!" the Punk told the Patient. "I took care of the whining little wimp, didn't I?" "We all know he was troubled as a youngster," said the Father. "His father tried talking to him, but he was always crying or yelling." "Yelling?" asked the Patient. "Yeah," said the Punk, "yelling. I wanted to kick their fucking faces in!" "He had a foul mouth," said the Mother, "that his mother smashed more than once." "And washed out with soap," added the Boy, afraid now of the Mother in Hazzard's Head, but desperately clinging to her nevertheless.

Indeed, Hazzard had been an unhappy and repressed child. But what does the Patient expect the Writer to make of it now, all these many years later? Something intelligible, illuminating and restorative?

"I simply want the Writer," said the Patient defensively, "to explain to the Lover why Hazzard is self-destructively obsessed with Marcelline Tatia." "That's simple," said the Paranoid. "It's because he's self-destructively obsessed with himself. He's been trying to do me in for as long as I can remember." "No, no," said the Punk, "he's obsessed with her because my cock needs exercise." "It's because I love her," said the Lover, the Boy adding, "It's because she's pretty like Mommy." "Oh, Christ!" cried the Depressive, throwing up his hands. "Just forget it."

Streetlamps and headlights shone everywhere on Columbus Avenue, which glistened with melted snow. Hazzard knocked snow from his cowboy boots and stepped into the vegetable market.

"Tomatoes," said the Mother. "I need a dozen of the Italian tomatoes." "There they are," said the Boy, pointing, as Hazzard picked up a plastic handbasket and moved to the display of tomatoes. He touched them carefully, the Mother checking for freshness and ripeness. "Tits," said the Punk. "They feel like little tits." "Soon," crooned the Lover, the Punk feeling Hazzard growing hard while bagging the tomatoes, hearing Marcelline in his head now: "Your cock's so hot, darling. I'm going to come for you. I'm going to come so much for you now!"

"I need a green pepper," said the Mother, "and parsley and garlic and two nice fresh leeks." "Shopping like a housewife," grumbled the Father, the Punk replying, "You talking to me?" "I'm only doing the shopping," the Son told the Father, "so the Lover can fuck her brains out." "Well," said the Father, "it's good to learn you're finally attracted to girls. Because for a time there I thought maybe the long hair and

tight pants meant . . ." "That you and the Mother had emas-
culated him!" shouted the Paranoid.

Hazzard stared absently into the handbasket.

"Salad greens," said the Mother. "What about pinto beans
for the chili?" asked the Son. "I've got them at home, dear."

Hazzard selected a head of Boston lettuce, a cucumber
(which the Punk, naturally, commented upon), a package of
sprouts, bunches of scallions and radishes.

"Finished?" said the Father impatiently. "What about
cheese?" said the Boy. "That's next door, honey." "And
next door to next door is the liquor store," added the Punk,
the Paranoid suddenly anxious, Hazzard desperately needing a drink.

"Are you really going to fuck her brains out?" the Boy
asked the Punk. "We're not going to fuck anybody's brains
out," said the Lover, "we're going to make love." "Yeah,
yeah," said the Punk, "but she only digs it if I fuck her brains
out." "That's right," said the Paranoid, "don't blame me for
what she makes the Lover do." "Can I watch?" asked the
Boy. "Sure, kid," said the Punk. "Stick around for the fire-
works."

Ten

DARKNESS had fallen fully by the time Hazzard had completed preparations for dinner. The Depressive always had his way with Hazzard at this time of night. The Punk, doing his darndest to get on top of the Depressive's assault, had downed half a pitcher of martinis. Drunk, he was having a good time at the expense of the Boy, who was setting the table as his mother had taught him.

"Well, well," said the Punk. "Where's your little apron, honey?" "So," said the Father, joining in, "Shirley still likes to play house."

Hazzard turned from the table and, lighting a cigarette, stared out the window.

The traffic on the avenue below had converted the once white snow to a filthy slush, and pedestrians crossing the street were forced to negotiate long detours round the puddles which swelled in the gutters.

"Why the hell don't she cook for me?" bitched the Punk to the Paranoid. "I mean, who the fuck ever heard of the guy cooking for the girl?" "Especially," said the exhausted Mother, "when she's such a tramp."

Hazzard was polishing off the puddle left in the pitcher of martinis when the phone rang.

"Ten bucks she's calling to cancel," the Paranoid bet the Lover.

Hazzard picked up on the third ring.

"Yes?" the Paranoid said suspiciously.

"I didn't wake you, did I?" His father sounded tentative and stilted.

"Wake me?" Hazzard said.

"I thought maybe you were napping."

"Uh-uh."

"Some weather we're having, huh? You don't run in this, do you?"

"Not today, no."

Hazzard struggled to think of something more to say, the Paranoid frightened by how much the Son still wanted to please his dad.

"What's new, Pop?" Hazzard said, lighting another cigarette.

"Not a thing. Same old crap. Just thought I'd check in."

"Well," Hazzard said, "I'm fine. Working hard. You going away after the first?"

"If I didn't have to take your mother I would."

"Go away by yourself then," Hazzard said, extinguishing the cigarette and listening to his father's despairing laughter.

"Are you kidding? She'd never let me."

"Oh, well," Hazzard sighed, "what else?"

"I don't know. Pick a subject."

"You called me, Pop."

"Because I thought maybe you wouldn't be in such a lousy mood for a change."

"I'm not in a lousy mood. I just don't like hearing about how unhappy you are."

"Better we should talk about how unhappy you are?"

"I just told you. I'm fine."

"Meet any nice girls lately?"

"No."

"Neither have I!"

"Very funny."

"So, how's the analysis? Working?"

"Little bit."

"I was thinking of seeing a shrink myself."

"Really? What for?"

"Are you kidding? So I can leave your mother already."

Hazzard cleared his throat. "Listen, Pop, I'm in the middle of cooking."

"Cooking? So how come you don't invite your mother and me for dinner already?"

"I told you. When I'm feeling better about things . . ."

"I thought you just said you're fine?"

"I lied."

"So, you're still mad as hell at me, is that it?"

"I can't talk now, Pop."

His father's voice suddenly drained of flippancy. "Jack, please, tell me what it is that I did that's so terrible that you can't find it in your heart to forgive me already."

"I really can't talk about this now. I'm sorry."

"Because I always thought we were close, you and me."

"We were."

"Let me ask you something here, Jack, without you getting mad as hell at me: Is it the psychiatrist who's telling you not to see us?"

"Psychiatrists don't tell you what to do."

"All right. Don't yell! Tell me, who's coming for dinner?"

"Marcelline."

"I thought you went to the shrink to get rid of her?"

"I did."

"So?"

"So *what?*"

"So I thought the girl was supposed to cook!"

Hazzard coughed. "I've got to go now, Pop. Take care of yourself."

"Did I say something wrong?"

"Chili's burning. Bye now, Pop."

"See us soon, Jack."

Hazzard set down the receiver and sat with his eyes closed for several minutes.

"Here comes a big wave!" cried his father, holding Jack, seven then, in his arms in the Atlantic. "Hold on, son."

"Hold me, Dad!" Jack hollered, cleaving to Dad, staring anxiously at the wave.

"Don't let go, son."

"I won't, I won't!"

The wave went over them, the son and his father, and they surfaced safely, Jack clinging, squirming, laughing excitedly, crying, "That was great!"

"See?" said his father. "See there, buster!"

"Thanks. Yikes, another one!"

"Want to try it alone? Go on. Let go, Jack. Let go, son."

"No, Dad, no! Please, don't let go. I'm scared."

"I've got you, buster."

"Thanks. Hold me, Marcelline."

"It's too warm, darling."

"Just for a while. Rub my forehead, please."

"You're just like a child, darling. Why are you crying?"

"Just a bad dream. Don't let go."

"You're so bizarre, my Jackie."

That winter when Jack was seven, his father took him sledding. Mr. Hazzard lay down first on the sled, and then Jack lay on top of his father's back, holding tightly to his father's shoulders and burying his small face in the back of his father's neck.

"Ready, Jack?"

"Ready, Dad. Yikes, it's steep."

"Hold on now. Don't let go."

"I won't."

"Here we go, buster!"

"I'm scared, Dad. Are you?"

"Nah!"

Jack shut his eyes against the wind and sparkling sunlight, Dad guiding the speeding sled to a slow stop, safe now.

"How was that, kiddo?"

"Great!" Jack pulling the sled, holding Dad's hand. "How come Mom didn't come?"

"I didn't ask her."

"Do you and Mom still love each other?"

"Sometimes."

"Do you love me and Mike, Dad?"

"I love you more than anything, Jack."

"I love you more than anything, too, Dad. Next I love Mike. Dad?"

"What?"

"I guess I love Mom but she scares me."

"She scares me too."

"Does Mom love me?"

"Very much."

"How come she wrecks my room and hits me with wooden hangers?"

"Your mom isn't always in control of herself. You have to try to understand."

"The chili's burning!" the Mother cried.

Hazzard hurried into the kitchen where the Lover stirred the bubbling beans before tasting them and adding a splash of wine.

Marcelline was late—as usual.

"I need another drink," said the Depressive to the Punk.

Hazzard prepared a fresh pitcher of martinis.

"Cheers!" the Lover said to the Punk.

"Something's burning again!" the Mother said.

"My balls," mumbled the Punk, who hated to be kept waiting.

The relief of the aspirin Hazzard ingested for his headache had just registered when the buzzer sounded.

The Lover checked himself in the hallway mirror before the Actor spoke into the intercom for Hazzard.

"That you?"

"It's me, darling."

He pressed the button to open the downstairs door. Then he hurriedly constructed a wigwam of logs in the fireplace, tossed in a match and, as the doorbell sounded, cued "Kind of Blue" on the stereo.

"You should have bought her some little flowers," the Mother said as Hazzard scooted down the hallway to open the door.

Marcelline stood before him now, her long auburn hair carefully combed, her blue eyes lined in black pencil, feline and frightening to the Recluse and the Paranoid, as she stood now in her fur coat, the shoulders dappled with glistening snowmelt, the Lover smitten as ever, the Depressive so sad when she was gone but anxious now that she was with him.

Hazzard smiled bashfully, and something mischievous and alluring flashed in Marcelline's eyes. She stepped inside and reached up on tiptoe to kiss him, Hazzard hearing the door

swing shut behind her, his arms around her, the fur wet, his
eyes and hers opening with their lips still touching.

"I missed you so much, darling."

"I missed you, too."

He stepped back, one hand holding hers.

"You keep getting prettier and prettier," the Actor said
for Hazzard.

"Only to keep you loving me more and more, my darling." Then she said, "Aren't you going to invite me in and
offer me a drink?"

When she tossed him the fur, he stood admiring her black
cashmere dress with the zipper up the back, the Punk meanwhile wagging his tongue lasciviously at the Lover as Marcelline moved into the living room to warm her hands before
the blazing flame.

The apartment was intimate now with the fragrance of her
perfume; and the martinis poured slowly from the icy pitcher
into the stemmed glasses. Hazzard presented Marcelline hers
as both stood facing the fire.

"Cheers!"

"Cheers, darling."

He finished the drink before turning to her, to stare at the
flames reflecting whitely in her gorgeous eyes—Circean
eyes, the Paranoid thought.

They sat down on the sofa adjacent to the fireplace.

"You are still so shy with me," Marcelline told him, touching his thigh, her nails there long and painted red.

"Good trip?" Hazzard said, leaning in to kiss her softly,
the Actor improvising, waiting for the Lover to become
stewed enough to play it fast and loose.

"I had a wonderful time. I love so much to travel." She
turned away a moment, then glanced around. "Where's
Harry?"

"Died last month."

"Oh, darling, I'm so sad for you. I know how much you loved that dog."

"More than anything," Hazzard said, the Boy inside crying, wanting comfort; but the Son remained quiet and removed in his distrust of Marcelline.

"I want to make you happy more than ever," Marcelline said.

The Depressive smirked at her pretension. "Long term or short term?" Hazzard said, the Punk's inveterate rage registering now as mordancy.

"Everything's short term!" Marcelline said impatiently. "Harry dying should have taught you that."

Hazzard returned his eyes to the fire. "How's your son?"

"I don't want to talk about my son."

"You went to court though?"

"I hate my ex-husband so much you wouldn't believe it."

"Actually, I think you still love him."

"I never loved him, darling." She pulled on her drink. "You know what? I showed him a photograph of you and he laughed."

"Laughed?"

"At your long hair. He was jealous at how young and beautiful you are. I told him you wanted to marry me and he was furious."

"I don't really want to talk about your husband," Hazzard said softly.

Marcelline sipped cautiously from her drink. "I thought about you all the time, darling. Kiss me."

They kissed, the drinks resting now on the end-table.

"You have some Quaalude for me tonight?"

"In my pocket."

"That's not a Quaalude," she said, touching, her mouth on

his, Hazzard feeling her breath on his face, growing harder beneath her touch.

"Give me," Marcelline said.

Hazzard halved the 'lude, knowing that, given the martinis, popping a pharmaceutical was like throwing gasoline on a burning house.

"The lewder the better," the Punk said for Hazzard, who winked as he handed Marcelline her share.

"I love when you're fun and crazy like this," she said, rinsing down the hypnotic.

"I know," he said, moving his hand slowly up her inner thigh.

"I had my legs waxed special for you."

"I can feel," he said, his hand moving now near her panties. "Lace," the Punk told the Father.

"Is the psychiatrist helping?"

"Helping me go broke."

"Do you talk to him about me?"

"I told you—sometimes."

"Tell me what you tell him."

"Guess," he said, his hand stroking slowly, the panties dampening.

"Do you tell him," she said biting his lip, "how much I love the way you fuck me?"

"I tell him how much I love the way I fuck you."

"Do you tell him how we watch each other sometimes?"

"M-hm."

"Tell me what else you tell him."

"Usually I tell him how lonely I feel when I'm with you."

"Everyone's lonely, you *stupido.* Love doesn't solve loneliness." Then she whispered, "Do you feel how wet I am for your cock?"

They kissed for a long time.

"Put a blanket on the floor, darling," she said languorously.

He spread the blanket on the floor, yanked off the lamp
and turned in time to see Marcelline step from her panties,
her heels still on, as he liked. He backed her away now from
the blanket, into the wall opposite the fireplace and lifted her
up. She responded by wrapping her legs around his waist and
gripping his shoulders as he pressed her back against the wall
with his chest while opening his zipper.

"You put it in," he told her, his interlocked hands forming
a cradle for her ass as he lowered and then raised her slightly
until she was impaled on him, her breath catching and then
imploding loudly as he rhythmically raised and lowered her.

"I love it so much the way you know how to make me
come so fast and good for you!"

When he felt her beginning to contract uncontrollably, he
speared more deeply.

"Oh, baby, I'm going to come for you, darling. Oh, it's so
good with you. Come with me, darling. Come inside of me."

Later, lying on the blanket with her, the Recluse and the
Teacher in Hazzard's Head were astonished at how much
importance the Punk and Lover assigned to such furious
ephemerality.

"It feels so good the way you eat my ass, darling."

"You want me to fuck you again?"

"You want that?"

"If you do."

"I want you to."

She rolled from her belly onto her back. Hazzard raised
and spread her legs, resting her ankles on his shoulders before pressing down on her beneath him, folding her in two
so that the heels of her shoes were forced behind her ears,
her eyes dreamy and a little afraid as he used his hand before

pressing in now slowly, Marcelline's eyes closing but her mouth opening, her tongue licking her front teeth as he thrust into her all at once, the Punk snickering in his head as Marcelline cried out, digging her long nails into his shoulder blades, though later she used her right hand to bring herself off concurrent with Hazzard, who exploded wildly, each of them breathless and perspiring and then very still.

"I love you so much right now, Jackie."

She kissed his nose as Hazzard pulled out entirely, rolling onto his back, very separate again, staring at the ceiling, Marcelline resting her face on his chest, curling herself into him, stroking his stomach.

"Jackie?"

"Huh?"

He worked to come back to her, the Punk in his inebriated head telling the Depressive, "You know what a broad wears behind her ears when she's having a ball? Her ankles!"

"No one makes love to me like that," she said. "I know from that that you love me so much."

He responded by massaging her small skeleton-sharp shoulders and pressing her to him. "Death!" the Paranoid whispered at the feel of the bones, the dazed Recluse longing to be left alone in peace in Hazzard's dreamy pharmaceutical narcosis. But now the Punk was telling the Father that if there were such a thing as the perfect broad she'd turn into a six-pack after you dicked her. "You see!" the Depressive said. "Nothing helps us. There's never any surcease."

Hazzard smelled marijuana and opened his eyes to behold Marcelline smoking a joint.

"Gimme," he said.

She put the joint to his lips and he inhaled.

"Did you sleep with anyone while I was away?" she asked.

"No," Hazzard said.

"I did."

"Good. Shut up."

"I hate to lie. I never lie. I love that about myself."

"Lie."

"Lying's stupid."

"Then shut up."

"Jackie?"

"Gimme."

She put the joint between his lips again.

"Jackie, I want to make love to you and another man."

"Forget it."

Some time later, Marcelline woke him. The flames of the fire had died to glowing embers. They drank coffee and smoked another joint before going into the bedroom to repeat what had worked so well in there many times before.

"I never let anyone else tie me up like this," she said, "except once."

Hazzard was unknotting her stockings from her wrists.

"I love to watch you coming on me," she said, tossing away the towel. "I want to watch you do that to someone else. Do you want to watch someone else do that to me?"

"I told you, Forget it."

"I hate when you're so boring and uptight."

"Tough."

"Are you falling asleep again?"

"Yes."

"I'm starving."

Starvation: Hazzard rolled away from her, his right arm folded in such a way beneath him that his hand pressed against the ribs that encaged his heart. The feel of his palm against this miraculous pumping muscle left him wondering why he had voluntarily pledged his allegiance to Marcelline Tatia with such emasculating effect. Starvation, he thought.

His naive heart was starving for the neurotic sake of his narcissistic head.

For the moment, however, feeling vanquished and very much afraid, he hungered only for the sanctuary of sleep. Muttering somewhat mordantly to Marcelline, "Chili's on the stove," he curled ever more tightly into his own confused flesh and bone for warmth.

Part Two

Part
Two

Eleven

WHEN Hazzard awoke in the morning, he moved immediately from the bed to the kitchen, where he listlessly smoked three Lucky Strikes in succession while staring through a window sheeted with ice. Outside, the slush had frozen in the gutters of the avenue in long gray piles left by the snowplows.

The sound of the bathroom door shutting registered just as he was slipping into sleep on the living room sofa. He prepared coffee; and coincident with the pot's last percolation, Marcelline appeared, already dressed.

"Morning," the Actor said as the Recluse drew his robe closed at the throat. The Lover felt silly standing before her dressed like the Boy in a bathrobe and sweatsocks, his teeth unbrushed, the Depressive, hung over, dying for the coffee which the Mother in Hazzard now poured.

"Coffee?" Hazzard said.

"I'm late, darling. I have business calls to make."

The Boy liked someone to talk to him in the morning.

"She's nice," the Boy told the Mother. "She rubs my tummy when I play with myself." "Send the bitch packing already," the Punk said.

"Have one cup," the Lover said, the Father in him wondering when the Writer intended to set to work today.

"It's too cold in here," Marcelline said.

She kissed him quickly before turning away and disappearing into the hallway. Hazzard heard the closet door open and hangers fall to the floor. Marcelline returned to the kitchen wearing her fur coat.

"How about a cup of chili?" Hazzard said, the Mother not seeing any humor in mocking her efforts of the previous day.

"Maybe tonight," Marcelline said, hugging him.

"Maybe late," he said. "I'm giving a reading at eight." The Lover was hopeful she'd evince some interest, but she parted from him in silence.

He followed her to the door to kiss her one last time.

"I love to miss you a lot," she said softly, her mouth against his, "and then fuck with you like last night. That's why I don't want to see you all the time. Try to understand."

"I'll be finished at ten," he said, the Paranoid afraid to ask her directly to attend the Writer's reading.

"Call me," she said.

Then she was in the hallway (at last, thought the Recluse), the click of her heels ringing as she descended the stairs and disappeared from view.

The Writer in Hazzard's Head watched her from the window adjacent to his desk as, below, she negotiated her way across the ice and snow on the sidewalk; and then he took his seat at the desk.

Since the aims of perverse sexuality are identical with those of infantile sexuality, the possibility for every human being to become perverse under certain circumstances is rooted in the fact that he was once a child.

For certain compulsion neurotics sexual intercourse unconsciously means a fight in which a victor castrates a victim. Men patients of this kind may have no other interest in sex than to get the reassuring proof that they are not the victim (it seems that they never can achieve a full reassurance). . . .

Twelve

HAZZARD'S physical development had been slow, or slower certainly than that of his friends. At thirteen, for example, Jack was the only boy in the "circle jerk" who didn't have pubic hair yet. This he discovered when he and his three friends had sequestered themselves in Joe's basement, where Blaine volunteered to show them how to do it. The object of the "jerk" of course was to win by coming first (Coming! Coming!), but Hazzard aspired simply to come like the other guys (who did have hair on their "hoses").

In fact, however, it would be another five years before Hazzard came, less from biological reasons than psychological ones (the Son was afraid of the judgments of the Mother and the Father in Hazzard's Head). In the intervening half decade, Hazzard would hear endless stories of "hand jobs" and "blow jobs" and "ream jobs" (as if these sexual activities might be part-time opportunities advertised in the employment section of the town paper). Moreover, for the life of him, Hazzard couldn't comprehend why Blaine and/or Joe would drive across interstate lines to a girl's house to "cop a feel" or "get a blow job." And why had Doyle suddenly ceased watching the New York Giants football games on television at Hazzard's house on Sundays and gone, instead, over to Donna's house, where he "ate her out" at halftime while she gave him a "hand job"?

Hazzard was confounded similarly by a game Blaine called "stinky finger," which Hazzard's friends played every Friday at midnight at The Diner, where they congregated to place their fingers before one another's noses before voting on who had the "stinkiest finger." Frankly, Hazzard was confused as to which and whose hole you put your finger in to make it "stinky."

"In her box, asswipe!" said Doyle, laughing at Hazzard and winking at Joe and Blaine who, laughing at Hazzard themselves, put their fingers to his nose and said, "So, who wins, hard on?"

Truth to tell, at fifteen Hazzard couldn't distinguish with any confidence between the meaning of "gash," "hair pie" and "noodle." Was each, for example, synonymous with "twat," "beaver" and "pussy"? And did you "eat out" her "gash" and "ream" her "A hole"—or what? Who copped a feel on whom? Even had he understood what this sexual arcana signified, even had he experienced a conscious desire to "get sucked off" or "dip his wick," the truth is, Hazzard probably would have stayed at home just the same. For his friends had hairy legs and hairy chests, and girls (according to Blaine Kisling) only dug guys who had hair all over them, which meant (naturally) that they had "big tools." According to Blaine, if a guy had a big tool then girls "creamed in their panties" and/or "popped their tampons."

Hazzard was just as happy to stay at home with his dog,

Mike, watching *The Fugitive* on television and eating pizza.
"Hey, asswipe," Blaine would ask Hazzard, "You jerk
off the dog or does the dog beat his meat while you
watch?"
"Hey, come on. What if my mom picks up the phone?"
"So? I wouldn't mind giving your old lady a poke. Ask her
if she digs me."
"Hey, shut the fuck up, okay?"
Hazzard had read every Hardy Boy book ever written and
never once had Frank or Joe Hardy, normal teenage boys (or
so they seemed to Hazzard), ever once "sucked titty,"
"eaten pussy" or "dicked a bitch." Neither Frank nor Joe
Hardy had ever "whacked off" eighteen times in one day
like Blaine Kisling said he had. In fact, like Hazzard himself,
neither Frank nor Joe Hardy had ever once whacked off.
    "What's the matter with you?" said his father. "Aren't you
attracted to girls?"
    At fifteen Hazzard visited an endocrinologist, who agreed
to administer hormone shots to facilitate Hazzard's growth
and physical maturation. Hazzard was relieved; he wanted
lots of hair on his penis and ankles so girls would "pop their
tampons" and let him drink a "Bloody Mary," like Blaine
wasn't too much of a pussy to do. Still, Hazzard worried that
such shots might make his penis "too big" (as his father's
purportedly had been for his mother). Indeed, the hormone
shots put hair on "Jack's pecker," as his father called it, but
Jack's pecker didn't get any larger; it simply sat in Hazzard's
underwear as unobtrusively and anonymously as Hazzard sat
in the dark at parties.
    Ironically, though Hazzard ceased wearing socks in order
to display his hairy new ankles, the girls he knew still seemed
to take greater interest in the burgundy-colored birthmark
on his lower lip. They were more interested, so Hazzard

thought, in encouraging him to have his birthmark removed by a laser beam than in encouraging Hazzard to remove their clothing so he could "cop a feel" or "finger fuck" them and perhaps win for once at stinky finger. Furthermore, it didn't help Hazzard's cause that his friends not only called him "fat lip" but, worse still, teased him relentlessly about taking off his shirt and showing everyone his pimply "pizza back"! It all induced Hazzard to stay home alone with his dog and listen to records while staring sullenly out the window, which, in turn, only inspired his father to ask him why he didn't ever go out on dates or see his friends anymore.

"Please leave me alone and close my door," became the refrain of the Recluse during Hazzard's teenage years.

"I'll leave you alone and close your door," his father replied, "as soon as you explain to me why you're not attracted to girls."

"Close the door, please. It's my room."

"It's my house, buster!"

Hazzard suffered his portion and began mirthlessly dating. In reaction to his dates' reactions to his birthmarked lip ("Did you get punched or kicked?" "Have you cancer or a herpes sore?" "Can't you have it *cut off?*" "Were you bitten or burned?" "Is that blood or what that makes it that color?"), Hazzard began to take girls to the movies (to remove his father's and his own doubts about himself), *where it was dark* and where, by sitting on their right side and staring straight ahead (even when talking) he could often avoid a discussion of the "birthmark" for at least one date, which was the only one to which he would *expose* himself.

"What happened to Sally?" asked his father. "Didn't you like her?"

"I bet," said his mother, "that she has bad breath like her father."

"Please leave me alone and close my door."

"Why do you always keep this door closed?" said his mother. "What do you do in here when *your* door is closed?"

"Nothing."

"Is that why all your pajama bottoms have holes in them?"

"Please leave me alone and . . ."

When he drove a date to the movie theater in his father's car, the girl would sit to his right, where she might see his birthmark ("fat lip," as his friends called it).

Hazzard, consequently, reflexively performed nervous gestures with his hands against his cheek to attempt to keep the birthmark hidden. Naturally, however, his nervous mannerisms only drew attention to his face, which he did his best to obscure by growing his hair long.

"Hey, Shirley," his father mocked, "when are you going to get your hair cut? Don't you think you look feminine with all that hair?"

"Please leave me alone and close my door."

"What the hell do you do in here all the time all alone?"

"Nothing."

"What happened to your friends?"

"They have girlfriends now."

"Do you?"

"No."

"Why not?"

"I don't know."

"Aren't you attracted to girls?"

"I guess."

"You guess!"

"Please leave me alone and close my door."

"Is there something you want to talk about?"

"No. I want to take a nap."

"Hey, what's that?"

"A story."

In one of his plays, N has a melancholic say: "If I could not annoy other people with my melancholia, I wouldn't enjoy it at all."

When Jack was sixteen and preparing to embark on his first formal date with Phyllis, a classmate from Ethical Culture who had invited him to her high school's freshman spring dance, Mr. Hazzard demonstrated to Jack how to kiss a girl goodnight. The classmate (a real "bowwow" as Hazzard told Blaine Kisling) lived in a nearby town, so Hazzard would have to be *driven* there. Hazzard had not wanted to accept the invitation, but he was afraid of what his father would think of him (and what he would think of himself) if he didn't accept the date; so he accepted. Moreover, Blaine Kisling told Hazzard that he should *definitely* go to the spring dance since, if the "bowwow" sucked his "dork," he could win the "Out of Town Blow Job of the Month Award." In preparation, therefore, for the "Big D" (date), Blaine provided Hazzard with a pornographic magazine which featured an article on "How to Make It Longer, Stiffer and Harder, and How to Keep It That Way Until She Does Something About It."

Although Hazzard decided to take Phyllis to the dance, it required one week's time for him to generate the courage to call her. Actually, since he was so anxious about speaking on the phone with Phyllis (his voice, when he was anxious, would suddenly disappear in a high thin whisper), he had written a script for himself to recite to Phyllis, which read, "Hello, Phyllis? Hi. This is Jack. Jack Hazzard. You know,

from Ethical Culture. I'm fine. How are you? Good. Listen, I'll go to the spring dance . . . if you still want to take me."
(!)

"So?" said his father, peeking into his room. "Are you going or not?"

"I don't know yet," Jack said, reviewing his script.

"Well, you'd better decide before dinner because your mother and I will go out if you don't need me to drive you."

"Please leave me alone and close my door."

"What's the matter now?"

"Nothing."

"All you and your mother do is mope."

"Hello?"

"Uh . . . Phyllis?"

"This is *her*."

"Uh . . . Phyllis . . . this is Jack. Jack Hazzard, the boy in . . ."

"I know. Can you come or not?"

"Uh . . . well . . .uh . . . yes, sure. I didn't call sooner because my dog was really sick and I had a sore throat."

"Do you have a tuxedo or not?"

"A tuxedo?"

"It's the rules. Listen, my mother gave me the address of a tuxedo place where you have to go. So write this down, 'k?"

"So?" said his father at the dinner table.

"I guess I'm going."

"This isn't the one," said his mother, "with the mousy-looking mother with the sagging breasts, is it?"

"I don't know," Jack said sullenly, eyes averted.

"Well," said his mother, "if it is, her mother's a real whore."

"What's wrong with that?" joked his father.

"Because Jackie's more like me than you when it comes to sex." (!)

"May I please be excused?"

"No, you may not."

"What's he crying about now?" asked his father, as Jack ran cursing to his room.

That Friday evening Hazzard anxiously dressed in the tuxedo his mother had helped him select from a rental men's-wear store before his father drove him to Phyllis's house. Jack sat silently, obediently holding the corsage that his mother had purchased for him to present to "his first real date!" (who, Hazzard hoped, would "suck him off" so he could win, for once, the "Blow Job of the Month Award" and be accepted as "cool" by his disgusting coterie of friends, who teased him cruelly about his lip, "pizza back" and "artificial" pubic hair).

As Hazzard prepared to leave the car to pick up Phyllis, he could see, through a picture window, Phyllis's mother (the real whore who probably had bad breath like Phyllis's father) calling to Phyllis, who, no doubt, was gargling upstairs in the bathroom (so she wouldn't have bad breath like her mother and/or father. Hazzard hoped his breath wasn't "bad").

"By the way," his father said as Hazzard started from the car, "when it comes to kissing Phyllis goodnight, all you have to do is give her a kiss on the cheek."

"I know," his son replied sulkily before closing the passenger door and anxiously approaching the "bowwow's" front stoop. (He wished he had stayed at home with Mike, a nice bowwow whom he wouldn't have to worry about forcing to blow him.)

The succeeding day Blaine Kisling said, "So?"

"So *what?*"

"You get the big bone in the small hole or what?"

"*What?*"

"You get sucked off or didn't you, asswipe?"

"Nothing happened," Hazzard said. "I danced, walked her back to her house, kissed her goodnight and hitched home."

"You cop a feel?"

"No."

"Dry hump her while dancing, at least?"

"No."

"Didn't you put the moves on the bitch?"

"No."

"Fag!"

Thirteen

"**S**HE came for dinner last night, but we never got around to eating," Hazzard told Dr. Roth now on the afternoon of the twenty-ninth of December.

"Tell me about it."

"It was very hot."

"Hot?"

"Yeah, hot."

"I'm afraid I don't understand what that means."

"Too bad for you," Hazzard answered, lighting a cigarette and looking away. "I had a dream I want to tell you about."

"Last night?"

"Yeah. I had a dream of my mother stripping. She used to do this strip routine for me."

"When?"

"There used to be this hit song, 'The Stripper.' I guess I was nine or ten. She would dance around the house, stripping."

"She removed her clothing during this routine?"

"In the dream?"

"When you were a boy."

"Not really. She would lower her blouse over her shoulder and purse her lips. Sometimes she'd hitch up her skirt while waving a long scarf at me."

"What was your reaction?"

"I'd laugh."

"And how did you feel?"

"Afraid, I guess."

"Go on."

"Also angry. She'd wave the scarf at me and I remember it made me really mad. My fists would close whenever the scarf touched my face."

"But you stood there laughing?"

Roth waited for Hazzard to resume, but he remained silent, staring meditatively at his knees.

"Where was your father during this strip routine?" Roth inquired.

"He wasn't in the dream."

"When you were growing up. Where was he then?"

"Working late, I guess."

"Was he working late when you were zipping up your mother's dress after watching her put on her face in her panties and bra?"

"I forget."

"You remember the panties though?"

"Please, don't provoke me."

"Surely you must remember where your father was."

"He was downstairs watching television."

"Tell me about your dad, Jack."

His father's boyhood dog's name was Tag.

"I loved Tag," said Mr. Hazzard to Jack, when his son was only a boy and had a dog of his own named Mike. "One time," Mr. Hazzard said, "I laughed at Tag after he ran into a tree while chasing a cat. That dog wouldn't look at me for three days! Some dog, that Tag."

"Did you love him like I love Mike?" Jack said.

"Sure. I was a boy, too, you know."

"Did you love your dad like I love you?"

"Hey, let's get washed up so your mother doesn't yell."

Another time his father told Jack how he cried the day Tag was hit by a car. Dad ran all the way to the vet's with Tag bleeding in his arms, and the vet stitched him up just in time.

"Nineteen thirty-four!" said his father wistfully, hands in his pockets.

"You saved him by running all the way?" said Jack, when he was eight years old in 1959.

"Yup."

"Were you fast, Dad?"

"Sure I was fast. I wasn't so chunky as a boy."

"Do you think I'm fast?"

"Sure you're fast!"

"Did your dad teach you to run like you taught me?"

"I wasn't too close to my dad."

"How come?"

"I was afraid of him."

"How come?"

"Hey, just let me read the headlines, okay?"

"Sorry."

In 1935 Tag went out the back door and never returned.

"Probably got run over or stolen," Mr. Hazzard said.

"Did you cry?"

"Sure I cried!"

"I'm sorry you cried, Dad," said his son, Jack, who was four years old when his father surprised him with a puppy.

"Thanks, Dad. Thanks."

"Do you like him?"

"He's great! Thanks! Thanks!"

"Come on then. I'll show you how to feed him."

"Great! Thanks!"

"Calm down, Jack."

"Sorry."

"Don't feed that dog in my kitchen!" screamed his mother, screaming year after year, "Get that dog off the bed! Put that dog in the basement! Don't bring that dog in the front door! Feed that dog outside! That dog made a mess in the basement!"

"Mike's sick, Mom."

"Don't talk back to me! Don't talk back to me! Go to your room!"

"Dad, how come Mom yells at me all the time?"

"Your mother's a sick woman, Jack."

"She scares me, Dad."

"She scares me, too, Jack. Now don't let her catch you with Mike on the bed."

"Okay," Jack whispered, kissing Dad goodnight. "Night, Dad."

"Night, son."

"Pat Mike goodnight, too."

When Mr. Hazzard patted Mike, Jack said, "Thanks, Dad. I love you."

"Go to sleep now."

"I love you, Dad."

"GET THAT GOD DAMNED DOG OFF THE BED!"

"Don't yell at him like that, Marion!"

Jack Hazzard's father was one of seven Jewish boys enrolled at the high school in 1937.

"They called me Jew boy," Mr. Hazzard told his son. "I

had to go to Newark for dates. The Gentile girls in the suburbs wouldn't date us."

"It must have been tough," said Jack, as they sat in the living room, Dad drinking his Scotch, Jack a Yoo-Hoo, Mike close too, no yelling now.

"Jew boy!" repeated Mr. Hazzard, shaking his head. "But your dad could fight, Jack. I never backed down from a fight —except with your mother!"

Jack laughed conspiratorially with his father, who glanced nervously over his shoulder toward the kitchen. "She must be cooking," his father whispered. Then: "Gimme a left jab and double up on the right hook!"

Jack danced gleefully round his father, earnestly flicking left jabs and stepping forward to throw the hook.

"Keep your head weaving when you step in with that hook. That's it. Thatta boy!"

"What are you two doing in there?" called Mrs. Hazzard from the kitchen.

"Nothing," said the father anxiously, winking at Jack, who winked back.

"Well, dinner's ready. Put the dog in the basement and wash up."

"Right," Jack called, faking a punch to his father and smiling. "Thanks, Dad. Thanks!" Jack hugging his father, clinging.

His mother now stood in the doorway. Jack could see the dementia in her eyes and recoiled from her.

"Are you teaching him how to fight?"

"He's good," his father said, thrusting his hands into his pockets, Jack wanting Dad to hit her, scare her back like she scared him.

"I've asked you a thousand times not to teach him how to fight."

"He might need to defend himself some day."

"We were just playing, Mom."

"Well, I haven't been playing. Dinner's getting cold."

He sat then in the kitchen all frightened and quiet, Mike in the basement whining, Jack mad deep down, mad and hating.

"Hurry up now and eat your dinner, Jackie. Mommy doesn't like being in the kitchen all night."

"It's real good, Mom."

"Don't talk with your mouth full, honey."

"Leave him alone, Marion!"

"Don't you tell me how to raise my son!"

Jack watched furtively, hoping Dad would punch and yell, scare her like she scared him. How come Dad just sat there?

Mr. Hazzard (Dad) might have gone to Princeton University but for his bad grades in French class. Had he taken summer classes, the administration would have accepted him, but Mr. Hazzard's parents wouldn't pay for the private summer lessons.

"It doesn't matter now," said Mr. Hazzard. "Things worked out, I guess."

Mr. Hazzard graduated from a local state college and entered the Army in 1943.

"Went in a private, came out a sergeant," his father said proudly to Jack, as they stood together in the attic one day in the autumn of 1963. Mr. Hazzard removed his sergeant's jacket from a hanger and held it open for Jack. "Go on, try 'er on for size."

Jack was only thirteen, but it fit him perfectly.

"I'd been sick before the war," Mr. Hazzard said. "Ninety pounds when I enlisted."

Jack's dad had contracted pneumonia in the summer of

1940 and by October the doctors said he wouldn't survive the night.

"I was in an oxygen tent. But I knew I couldn't die because I hadn't been laid yet!"

Jack and his father laughed together then in 1963, when Jack didn't exactly know what "laid" meant, although his friends were starting to "cop feels" and "get sucked off," so Hazzard assumed it was something "dirty like that."

"You almost died?" Jack said, astounded. "What happened?"

A doctor experimented with a sulfa drug never before administered to a human being, and miraculously it saved Jack's dad's life.

"It was in all the papers," Mr. Hazzard said, showing Jack a clipping from the *Newark News* he'd kept in a trunk in the attic. "It was a last-ditch thing. They'd only used the sulfa drug on rats before me. But it saved my life. Then I met your mom. Then you were born."

Jack stood before his father in the attic in his sergeant's jacket and dashed his eyes.

"Hey, don't get upset. I didn't die. Come on. Let's show your mother how you look in the jacket."

"Hey, Mom!" Jack cried, running down the stairs to show his mother how he fit into his father's sergeant's jacket.

But his mother was in bed with a migraine headache.

"What is it, Jack? I was sleeping."

"Nothing. Sorry." Closing the door carefully, the room smelling funny.

"I had an affair once," Mr. Hazzard said, "and your mother found out."

"An affair?" Jack said, age fourteen. "What's an affair exactly?"

"Well, it's when you fall in love when you're married, with someone to whom you're not married."

"Was she pretty like Mom?"

"Not really."

"How come you fell in love then?"

"She was nice to me, I guess."

After the war, Mr. Hazzard, who weighed at twenty-two no more than his thirteen-year-old son, fell in love with Lori Hood. He proposed to her in the spring of 1947.

"What happened then?"

"Well, in those days you had to get permission from the girl's dad. I asked her father and he said I didn't make enough money to support his daughter in the fashion she was accustomed to."

"Really! Did you punch him out?"

"Of course not."

"What happened then?"

"I guess I figured after a year in the shoe business I'd be making enough money and receive her dad's permission. But after six months Lori became engaged to another man."

"Did you cry?"

"No, I didn't cry. Because things have a way of working out. A year later I met your mom."

"You mean you loved somebody else before you met Mom?"

"Yes."

"Did she let you tongue kiss?"

"Sure."

"You loved Mom but she didn't let you tongue kiss?"

"I don't think I ever really loved your mom."

"You didn't?"

"What are you two whispering about?" Mrs. Hazzard said,

entering the room bad-temperedly, holding a stack of laun-
dry.

"Men's talk," Jack said proudly.

"Well, go wash up and put the dog in the basement. Dinner's almost ready."

After his mother had left the room, Jack whispered, "So
after Lori you got engaged to Mom?"

"Prettiest girl I'd ever met," he told Jack as they walked
to the bathroom to wash up.

"Mom or Lori?"

"Your mom."

"Was Lori pretty?"

"I guess."

"Supper's getting cold," his mother called.

"Do you still love Lori? Is she the woman you had an affair
with?"

"Come on, your mother's waiting."

"Do you still love Lori?"

"Hey, do you think you can shut up for five minutes?"
Shame filled Jack's chest and he turned to the wall, crying
like a sissy, he told himself.

"Now damn it, son, you're going to get me in trouble by
talking as much as a woman."

Dashing his eyes, Jack said, "Sorry, Dad."

"Are you going to leave Mom like you said last night when
she was screaming?" Jack asked, fifteen then, and alone in the
living room with Dad.

"I couldn't do that. It would break my mother's heart."

"What are you two whispering about?"

"Nothing, sweetheart."

"Well, dinner's almost ready."

When his mother returned to the kitchen, Jack said, "What about my mom's heart?"

"You see," Mr. Hazzard said, "when I was your age, when I was fifteen, my mother came to me and said she was leaving my father."

"Pop-pop?"

"That's right."

"Did you cry?"

"Heck, no."

"How come I always do?"

"Because you've got your mother's genes. Anyway, I begged her not to leave my father. She gave in. I guess I've always felt I owed her one."

"What do you mean?"

"She's begged me not to leave your mother."

"Does Mom know?"

"Are you crazy?"

"DINNER'S READY!"

"We're coming!"

"We're coming!"

"Get that damn dog out from under my dining-room table!"

"Don't shout, for Christ's sake!" shouted his father.

"Then take your hands out of your pockets for once and help me serve this hot food I spent five hours preparing!"

"You want a God damn medal!"

Jack started to cry, even at fifteen, as his mother hurled the food to the floor, the trays crashing, Dad saying, "Are you crazy, Marion?"

Glancing at the clock, Dr. Roth said, "I'm afraid we'll have to wait until tomorrow to pursue this further. Meanwhile, good luck at your reading tonight."

"How'd you know about that?"

"Your picture's in the centerfold of the *Village Voice.*"

"You read the *Village Voice?*"

"No one mentioned the picture to you?"

Hazzard stood, perplexed.

"Marcelline coming to the reading?" Roth inquired.

"I haven't really asked her."

"Planning to?"

"I don't know," Hazzard said, feeling his hands sliding into his pockets.

"Well, enjoy yourself."

Fourteen

HAZZARD called her from a street-corner phone booth after stopping at a newsstand. There was the Writer, Hazzard's portrait from his second novel in the centerfold of the *Voice*.

Snow swirled swiftly into the rows of roaring traffic as Hazzard spoke excitedly.

"Hey—get this! My picture's in the paper."

Marcelline sounded tired. "What paper?"

"The *Voice!*"

"You woke me. I was sleeping."

"Really? It's three o'clock."

"I was up late with my lover taking drugs."

"I just thought I'd tell you I was in the centerfold of the *Voice*."

"What for?"

"I'm giving a reading at the New School tonight. You want to come?"

"I can't hear you, darling."

Hazzard shouted above the acceleration of a bus. "You want to come to a reading I'm giving tonight?"

"They took your picture because you're reading from your book?"

"My new one. You want to come?"

"I love it when you make me come, darling."

"Seriously. To my reading. You want to?"

"People sit and listen to you read?"

"Unless there isn't enough room and they have to stand."

"I never even heard of the *Voice*."

"You never heard of the *Village Voice?*"

"Oh. *Merda,* there's my other phone."

"You want to come or not?"

"I don't know. I'll call you back, darling. Ciao."

By six Marcelline had failed to phone. To keep the Depressive and the Punk from losing their cool, the Actor had taken to drinking before Hazzard phoned her.

"What time is it?" Marcelline said.

"Six."

Hazzard could hear her television playing in the background.

"Well," she said, yawning languorously, "First I was on the phone to L.A. Then London."

"You'll have quite a phone bill."

"Don't start with me!"

"You coming to the reading or not?"

"I can't."

"I guess I should have mentioned it sooner."

"It's not that, darling. I'm just not in the mood tonight. I'm bored and feeling crazy. I want to take drugs and go dancing."

"Well, I have to shake a leg myself."

"I'm going to the Paradise Garage. It's mostly black men there. I'll find us a cute one."

Hazzard hung up at once and stalked into the bathroom for a Valium to govern the chorus of voices that commenced at once. He was washing down the pill with a shot of vodka when the phone rang.

"I knew she'd call me back," the Lover said, relieved, the Punk hollering, "I'll kill the bitch the next time I see her!" "That's precisely what I'm afraid of," the Paranoid told the Recluse as the Actor in Hazzard answered the phone without saying a word.

"Hello?" The disembodied voice wasn't Marcelline's.

"Yes?" Hazzard answered apprehensively.

"Hello, dear," his mother said. "Hold on a second, please."

Hazzard heard the phone drop, the Depressive mumbling, "Just hang up." "No!" cried the Boy, jubilant to hear from his mother. "I'll handle this," the Actor told the Patient.

"I'm so sorry, dear, but things are just crazy around here at the moment."

She sounded a little breathless now, her voice upbeat in that musically dissembling way, his mother (like himself) always at the mercy of swiftly shifting moods, never really present, her eyes either dead or wildly effervescent, the emotional switches within either overloaded or off, either all dressed up and frenetic or comatose in her bathrobe, rings under her eyes, looking to find something Jackie had done wrong.

"I can only talk for a moment," Hazzard said.

"Not on the counter," his mother was telling someone now, no doubt the maid. "Hello, dear. I'm so sorry."

"What can I do for you, Mom?"

She was telling him now that his father's birthday was the
day after tomorrow and wouldn't he just this once agree to
meet with them for a celebration drink since he hadn't seen
them in—what? over a year now, and it really would make
Daddy so happy if Jackie surprised him.

"I don't know, Mom. I'm awfully busy this week."

"Surely," his mother said, "you could spare just an hour
on Saturday night. We'll be at Joe Allen's for dinner. I can't
tell you how much we've missed not seeing you, Daddy
especially."

Hazzard lit a cigarette. "I'll try my best to be there, okay?"

"I'll expect you at six-fifteen. That will give us plenty of
time."

"How's Dad doing?" Jack said, the Patient permitting the
Son one question.

"Frankly, not so well, dear. He's getting on in years. He's
going to be sixty-seven, you know, and his business is falling
off. He's working himself half to death and the rest of the
time he worries about you. I can't begin to explain how your
refusal to see us has crushed him."

"I think you just did," Hazzard said.

"Well, dear, I know very well that you haven't asked for
my opinion on this subject, but I really do think you should
be mature enough now to find a way to work things out
between yourself and your father and me, because however
imperfect we might have been and no doubt still are, we are
your parents."

"Listen, Mom," the Actor said assertively, "I can't go into
this right now."

"I just think it's time you stopped trying to deny our
existence."

"Mom, I said I'll see you Saturday at six-fifteen. Let's leave
it at that."

"All right, then, dear. I'll look forward to seeing you."

"Likewise."

"Even though I'm scared to death of you."

"Mom, I've got to run. I'm late."

"Goodbye, dear."

Hazzard had knotted his tie and slipped on his tweed sports jacket when the phone rang again. He studied himself in the long mirror bolted to his bedroom door, the Mother in him wondering if he should be wearing jeans and cowboy boots with the jacket and tie. "It's my reading," said the Writer to the Son, "I'll wear whatever the hell I want." "Maybe you should change your pants," the Paranoid suggested, the Depressive ignoring them all, apathetic, at best, after all these years, to Hazzard's behavior, as it only engendered one conflict or another.

"Hello," Hazzard said.

"Are you angry at me?"

The way Marcelline pronounced "angry" made the word sound like "hungry"; but Hazzard wasn't inclined to reconsider his crisis of starvation.

"I'm way late," he said.

"Don't be mad at me, darling."

"I'm not mad. I'm on my way out."

"Listen, my darling, I have to meet a client at a gallery opening. But I want to see you later."

"Meet me for dinner then," Hazzard said calmly, staring into his reflected eyes, the Lover assuming command of the Actor.

"Where?"

"At the Indian joint on East Sixth Street. Ten o'clock okay?".

"I'll try."

"I'm afraid I'll need a yes or no."

"Don't be so bossy. I'm not your wife."

"I'm just asking you to make up your mind, not telling you how to."

Marcelline laughed, her voice easy now.

"Sometimes I love it when you're bossy. I don't like to always have my way with you."

"Please, Marcelline. I'm late. What'll it be?"

"What'll it be?" she mimicked him; but then she said softly, "I'll see you at the Indian *joint,* my bossy darling."

"Swell! *Salud!*"

"I love you, Jackie."

"And I love you."

Fifteen

THE cab ride to the reading reminded the Boy in Hazzard's Head of the Wild Mouse amusement-park ride at Coney Island. Hazzard left the window open to steady his nerves, the cold air tranquilizing the Writer's increasing edginess, which the Actor couldn't understand. "Of course you can't understand," the Paranoid told him. "Because you don't mind making a fool of yourself." "It's an audience, isn't it?" the Actor snapped, working against the wind to keep Hazzard's hair in place. "Audience?" the Recluse inquired anxiously, and Hazzard felt his nerves start to give out on him. "Don't do this to me, sweetheart," the Writer implored the Depressive.

Upon his arrival, book collectors approached him in the lobby for autographs to the first edition of his latest work, which only further unnerved the Recluse and the Paranoid, neither of whom could understand the Writer's sudden ebullience; and the next thing Hazzard knew, he was seated on stage as his educational background and previous fictional works were catalogued respectfully by the moderator, whose words elicited polite applause from the auditorium audience of several hundred, as did Hazzard's half-hour reading.

"I'm famous!" the Boy told the Mother, as the Actor smiled shyly at the audience for Hazzard upon completion of the Writer's reading.

"I always knew you'd be famous!" the Mother said, massaging the Boy's tushie lovingly. "Do you like me a little now?" the Son asked the Father, who, reading the stock-market page, said obliviously, "Just let me finish up here." "Face it," the Writer told the Patient, "I'm the only redeeming quality in Hazzard's Head." "Too bad I'm not impressed," the Depressive said. "About what?" the Father asked, folding the paper. "Oh, nothing," the Son sulked.

The applause abated and ceased.

During the subsequent question-and-answer period, the Actor did his best to respond with a droll insouciance which the Recluse found supercilious and the Patient considered condescending. "I'm protecting us," the Actor told the Paranoid.

"Are you a Vietnam veteran?" someone asked.

Hazzard was nonplussed. "No. Why do you ask?"

"You seem so angry. I mean, your work does. I thought perhaps the war had scarred you."

"No," Hazzard said. "My enemies abide within."

The moderator pointed to the rear of the auditorium.

"Your characters all seem defeated by life. Do they represent your world view? Are you, that is, as defeatist as they about the possibilities life affords?"

"World view?" the Boy said, frowning. "I just like playing with words."

"No," Hazzard replied, and considered leaving his answer at that; but the Writer overruled the laconic Son. "I prefer,"

Hazzard resumed, "to think on some of my characters as despairing rather than defeated. Defeated people—or defeated characters, rather—have ceased to struggle; and without struggle there's no conflict; and, as we all know, without conflict, there's no story."

"Blow it out your ass!" the Punk told the Writer.

"Your fiction, then, concerns characters struggling against despair?"

"Yes," the Depressive answered simply for Hazzard.

"What's it like to be a writer?" someone else inquired.

"Lonely," the Recluse answered.

"Why do you write then?"

"To keep myself company." The Boy this time, the Actor in Hazzard smiling.

"Isn't that a contradiction?"

"Absolutely!" The Depressive in him.

"Be less droll," the Mother castigated the Actor. "Charm them," the Father advised. "I want to get the hell out of here," the Recluse told the Depressive. "The less I say," the Paranoid told the Mother, "the less the Father will criticize us." "That's right," said the Father, "Just don't talk as much as a woman for once!"

"Would you say a person has to be a little crazy to become a writer?"

"Not necessarily," the Actor answered for Hazzard. "But it can't hurt."

Fearful of this flippancy, the Mother coerced the Paranoid to signal to the moderator that Hazzard didn't want to answer any more questions.

Thus Hazzard was thanked on behalf of some committee or other, and polite applause issued from the audience as Hazzard left the stage. To the Lover, the anticlimax of watching the auditorium empty was redolent of the post-coitus *tristesse* of another kind of ordinary performance.

Naturally, the Paranoid was absolutely mortified by Hazzard's comportment.

"Good Christ," he complained to the Father. "He's always making me look like some kind of sophomoric smartass!" "Don't remind me," said the Depressive, the Son asking the Father, "What'd I do wrong?" "Better question," said the Father, "would be, Why can't you do anything right?" "I thought he did just fine," said the Patient. "Sure you think that," said the Punk. "You're a mental case!"

Hazzard lit a cigarette while exiting the empty auditorium with the moderator, who thanked him again before shaking his hand and disappearing down a narrow side corridor. Hazzard turned to the exit doors at the far end of the lobby.

A woman appeared to be waiting for him. At first he didn't recognize her with her brown hair cropped close to her face and her small body bundled in a blue woolen coat. But when he realized who it was, he froze in his tracks, and blood drained from his face.

Sixteen

DURING Jack Hazzard's last year of graduate school, he had cohabited with Jill Downs, a serpentine young woman who possessed such a joyful attitude toward life that the Lover and the Boy nicknamed her "Jolly." Of course, not all the inhabitants were unanimous in their approbation of her. The Recluse, for example, wanting only to be left alone, found her continuous presence difficult to tolerate. And the Punk resented Hazzard's fidelity to her. Consequently, after two years together, the Depressive began to sulk and the Punk and the Father to carp mercilessly at her, peevishly criticizing Jill Downs for not watering the plants properly, for forgetting to vacuum under the sofa (as the compulsive Mother in Hazzard always did when he vacuumed), or buying tangerines instead of the Sunkist navel oranges the Son loved.

And then, after living with Hazzard for three years, Jill was pressured by her parents either to marry Jack Hazzard or to leave him.

"All right," Hazzard acceded one day in November when he was twenty-seven. "Let's tell them we'll do it."

Hazzard rather suspected the Lover's submission was a mistake, but, given the powerful influence of the Son's guilt upon the Depressive, the Writer found it impossible to over-rule the Lover's compliance with, and the Actor's commit-ment to, an engagement. Naturally, the Father and Mother in Hazzard's Head were thrilled by the Son's sudden "matu-rity." The Lover, frankly, didn't understand the purpose of such a formality, since he and Jill were happy with their informal arrangement; but he, too, acquiesced, believing, as did the Son, that marriage, after three years of living together, was, as the Father contended, "the right thing to do."

Since Hazzard repressed his feelings, problems regarding the engagement commenced to torment him privately. The Punk, for example, felt that marrying Jack's first real girl-friend was depriving him of all the "pussy, gash, twat, beaver and hair pie," about which he'd always dreamed when younger, but which (since the Son was repressing certain forbidden impulses) Hazzard had felt prohibited from "eat-ing, fingering and fucking," to employ the Punk's verbiage. In fact, by complying with the engagement to Jill Downs and then holding in his reservations, the Punk in Hazzard's Head became nearly deranged with rage, for marriage would re-quire fidelity ("Says who?" asked the Father), and without new sexual conquests the Punk would have no way of abating the Son's tormenting sense of sexual inadequacy by perpetu-ally demonstrating to the Father, via the Lover, that Haz-zard's womanizing was proof of his virility and sexual confidence. The Paranoid, on the other hand, terrified of the sadistic sexual impulses of the Punk, depended on the Re-cluse to protect Hazzard from all sexual engagements by way of a severe and punitive isolation from the world. In either case, Jill Downs was a problem.

Once again the Depressive offered the only solution: depression.

Consequently the Lover admitted to a degree of sexual dissatisfaction with Jill Downs. "I started getting the hots for other women," the Punk remembered. "Shame on you," said the Mother, recommending that he hold in his true feelings. "But I would never have cheated on Jill," said the Lover. "Because I loved her," said the Boy. "You idiot!" snapped the Depressive. "I can't love anyone. Not even Hazzard himself!" And so it was the Depressive who marshaled the wills of many of the inhabitants of Hazzard's Head against the Son's decision to marry Jill Downs.

"On the other hand," the Father argued, "the real value of marriage is that you've always got your wife to blame for your unhappiness." "He didn't need a wife," the Patient told the Father, "he's had you."

And the Boy had cried, giggling, "The Son's married to Daddy!"

The Punk began to rage mercilessly at Jill Downs, Hazzard yelling and screaming about petty matters.

"He acts just like Mommy," the Boy said.

The Depressive, like Hazzard's mother, began to suffer headaches and long bouts of gloomy and hateful silences, the Recluse remaining in Hazzard's study, staring out the window, as the Son had done when Hazzard was younger.

"What's wrong, sweetheart?"

"Don't come in here without knocking!"

"I did knock. You mustn't have heard. Would you like some tea?"

"What I'd like, Jill, is to be left alone, thank you."

"Don't be mean to her!" cried the Boy, the Son and the Lover; the Punk and the Depressive replying, "Fuck off!" as the Father added, "You've got to show a woman who's boss. You hear, son?" "What?" said the Son, who, waging a war of survival (in Hazzard's Head) against the Mother and the Father, realized that the battle had spread out there again, not only to his mother and father but to his prospective mother-in-law and father-in-law. Consequently, as ardently as the Mother and Father protested against terminating the engagement, they were easily outvoted by the other inhabitants of Hazzard's Head. The Boy, who had loved Jill Downs with simplicity and trust, was crushed by the breakup of Jack and Jill, which occurred six months after she and Hazzard had announced the engagement.

As they shook hands now, after the silence of a five-year separation, Jill Downs said, "I saw your picture in the *Voice* and couldn't resist."

He lowered his eyes ashamedly and sorrowfully to behold the Frye boots she'd bought one Saturday seven years ago when they'd gone shopping together after ice-skating.

"May I hug you?" he asked tentatively, releasing her hand and gazing into her face.

"Sure," she said, smiling.

When his arms went around her shoulders and the side of his face touched hers, the Lover remembered a million things reflexively, so that the Actor lost control and Hazzard's throat constricted as tears welled in his eyes.

"You jerk," Jill said affectionately as they separated and Hazzard shielded his remorseful eyes by bowing his head. "I wanted to marry you!" the Boy screamed, silently and invisibly to her. "But the Depressive and the Punk wouldn't let me. I still love you! Remember me?"

"I hope I haven't done the wrong thing," Jill Downs said.

"Of course not," he said softly, dropping his cigarette and extinguishing it with his boot.

"I really enjoyed the reading," she said. "You're not as funny as before, but you're much more honest."

The Boy in Hazzard couldn't refrain from hugging her again, although the Recluse and Paranoid tried.

"I've thought about calling you a million times," the Lover and the Boy had him say.

"I wish you had."

Jill gently stepped away and pulled nervously at her hair. "Don't stare," she said. "I know you must hate it."

"No, I like it."

"Liar. You always lied to be polite."

"Really!" he insisted, lying.

"Look how long yours is!" She laughed in that explosive, exuberant way that had always made the Boy in Hazzard laugh too.

Hazzard laughed. "Jolly!" The Boy screamed. "Jolly!"

"You haven't changed a bit, have you?" she said.

"Why does that sound like an indictment?"

She studied his face, remembering. "I thought I'd feel like a stranger with you, but I don't. I've missed you, Jack."

"I've missed you, too," he answered, desperately looking for somewhere to look. And then he said, "I'm sorry I behaved so unforgivably."

"It was quite forgivable. I shouldn't have pressured you about marriage."

Hazzard lit another cigarette.

"I suppose," he said, "it's too late to pretend five years never happened?"

Jill lowered her gaze.

"I heard you were living uptown," she said nervously.

Hazzard nodded and exhaled smoke rings.

"How about you?" he said. "I heard you were in the Village."

"Not anymore," she said. "I've moved to a loft in Tribeca. I got married last spring."

Hazzard felt blood filling his face. The Actor tried to posture cavalierly but couldn't. "Well," Hazzard said reflexively, "congratulations."

"How about you?" she asked.

"Oh, mostly hit-and-run stuff, as the saying goes."

Jill frowned, then referred to her wristwatch. "I'm late for a dinner party."

"So am I."

They walked together through the exit door and into the cold wind funneling down Fifth Avenue.

Hazzard raised the collar of his coat as Jill signaled for a cab.

"Maybe," Hazzard said cautiously, as the cab halted, "we could have lunch together sometime?"

"Maybe," she said, and then, taking his hand, recanted. "I don't think we should."

Hazzard said he understood and opened the cab door for her.

"Alas," Jill Downs said, "goodbye, sir."

"So long, Jolly."

She blushed at the mention of the nickname he'd given her back then.

After she kissed him quickly goodbye, she said, "If I change my mind, I'll call you."

"Please," Hazzard said.

She closed the door and leaned forward to give the driver the address.

Hands in his pockets, Hazzard watched the cab turn the corner and disappear completely.

Seventeen

HAZZARD walked east along brightly lighted Tenth Street, the branches of the trees and the window ledges of the brownstones shimmering like silver with frozen slivers of snow. The abandoned Bowery, however, was entombed in darkness, the only light leaping as flames from trashcan fires around which homeless men huddled to keep warm. Hazzard hurried into a Second Avenue deli and purchased two quarts of beer before shuffling down the icy sidewalk of Sixth Street toward a neon sign flashing "Nirvana."

In response to the front door's tinkling of bells, a young Indian man came from the kitchen.

"Yes, please?"

Hazzard blew into his fist to relieve the chill in his chest.

"Table for two," he said.

"Anywhere you wish, please."

Jack chose a table away from the draft and drank beer while waiting for Marcelline.

His mother was another one who always kept him waiting; especially after school when he was little and she'd promised to be on time if it was raining; but she never was, and Jack, wet and mad, gave her the silent treatment because if he yelled she'd crack his fresh mouth.

Ten-fifteen: Even when he was late, Marcelline managed to be later.

Sometimes, when Daddy worked late on Friday nights, Jackie ate dinner alone with his mother.

"I shall always believe," his mother told him (once if a million times when they were eating alone), "that I was conceived accidentally when my mother was sixteen and that my father would never have married her had he not unintentionally impregnated her."

"Only sixteen!" Jack said, when he was twelve and his father was working late at the shoe store one Friday night.

"That's right, dear. I was conceived illegitimately when my mother was a high school sophomore. My father dreamed of being a pharmacologist but wound up a candy-store owner . . . due to me."

"Don't cry. It wasn't your fault."

"I grew up feeling as if I'd done something terrible to them, Jackie. I wasn't raised by a loving mother and father who catered to my every wish and whim like you . . . yours . . . do."

"When's Dad coming home?"

"Daddy's working late. You know, honey, I've always dreaded not being a good mother to you. I am a good mother, wouldn't you say so?"

"I guess. Can I call the store and see if Dad's left yet?"

"You mustn't bother Daddy at work."

"Can I watch TV now then?"

"*May* I watch TV."

"*May* I watch TV now then?"

"Yes, you *may.*"

"Can I get Mike from the basement so he stops whining?"

"No, you *may* not."

"Can I take the TV into the basement then?"

"There's your father now! Hello, Daddy!" cried Mrs. Hazzard, for Jack's mother called Jack's father "Daddy" and Mr. Hazzard called Jack's mother "his big girl."

"How's my big girl and my little boy?"

"How's Mommy's soup?"

"Great!"

"Smile for a minute, Jackie."

When Jack had smiled, sticking out his tongue foolishly, his mother said, "Are you brushing your teeth, dear?"

"Yes," her son said nervously, recoiling into himself in preparation.

"Then why are your teeth all yellow?"

"I don't know," Jack said, ashamed, averting his eyes.

"As an infant," Mrs. Hazzard said (as Jack stared out the window while eating soup on a Friday night when his father was working late), "I had my legs bound together in my cribby by my mommy. I was taught at a very early age that a good girl keeps her legs closed."

"May I be dismissed from the table now, please?"

"Not if you're going to go to your room and close the door."

"Why can't I close my door? It's my room."

"Because it's *my* house, honey. There's Daddy!"

"So," said Mr. Hazzard (their daddy), "what did you two do today that I should know about?"

"He let the dog jump on his bed and get the blanket all dirty," his mother said. "I spent all day washing."

"She did not!" Jack countered uselessly. "She blabbed on the phone. And Mike just jumped up once. Mom's lying!"

"Don't you raise your voice like that, young man."

"No party tonight, Jack?" his father said, changing the subject. "No girls?"

"Jackie's only thirteen," said his mother. "He's got more important things on his mind."

"May I be dismissed from the table, Mom?"

"To do what?"

"Go to my room, I guess."

"Hey, don't you want to sit and tell me what you accomplished today?" his father said.

"I just want to go to my room with Mike and listen to music, okay?"

"Not with the dog, Jackie!"

"And don't play that crap too loud, son."

"What's he crying about now?"

"Hey, son, come on. Is it girl problems? She's got a date with another guy, right?"

"Don't you walk away cursing at your mother and father, young man!"

"I adored my father," Mrs. Hazzard said to Jack, on a Friday night when Mr. Hazzard was working late again while Jack sat at home listening again to another self-absorbed soliloquy by his mother (who frightened him and from whom Jack wanted his father to protect him). "He was an incurably weak man," Jack's mother said of her father, "who allowed my mother to abuse him and me. He never protected me or any of my younger brothers and sisters from her. She controlled all of us, dear. Are you listening to me, Jackie?"

"What?"

"I truly believe that my father died of a broken heart. What's so fascinating out that window?"

"What?"

Her father, she told Jackie, suffered from dementia praecox. "He was strange, just like you, dear."

Depressions afflicted him. At the dinner table (she told Jackie at the dinner table), he (her father) would unexpectedly begin to sob. Many times Mrs. Hazzard's mother would find Mrs. Hazzard's father (Jack's grandfather) praying in his pajamas in the woods late at night during rainstorms.

"He was suicidal," said Mrs. Hazzard, who was suicidal herself (like the Depressive in Hazzard's Head). "He would lock himself in the bathroom and threaten to slash open his wrists. One time I had to phone the police. They broke down the door, dear, and found him sitting on the potty with doo-doo in his pants crying into his hands. After that my mother had all the doors removed. I had to make my pee-pee and doo-doo in a room without a door."

"May I be excused now?"

"Jackie, you open that door for Mommy!" his mother hollered on a Saturday afternoon after Mommy and Daddy had been yelling again, Jack going to the bathroom, locking the door.

"Quit screaming at him!" Daddy's voice there now.

"Jackie, this is your mommy, honey. What are you doing in there to yourself?"

"Damn it, Jack. Open the door now, son. You're upsetting your mother. Everything's fine now."

"No!"

"I'm going to call the police, Jackie!"

"Jack, you open the door, son!"

"Leave me alone!"

"All right, young man, I'm calling the police and they'll put you in jail!"

When Jack Hazzard was seven his mother developed migraine headaches which persisted, at regular intervals, for twenty years.

"It's probably the birth-control pills Daddy makes me take," said Mrs. Hazzard, accepting a tray of tea and toast from her son, Jackie.

"Can I put some lights on downstairs now? It's dark."

"Light hurts my eyes, dear."

"But you're in your room."

"It seeps under the door."

"When's Dad getting home?"

"He's working late during Christmas week. This is the wrong jam."

"I'm sorry."

"I'll try to get up myself in a little while and get the proper jam."

"I'll get it, I'll get it."

"Thank you, dear."

Hazzard's mother phoned the police department one night in winter when Jack was eleven after Jack's father ("working late," purportedly) had failed to return home by 3 A.M.

"Is something wrong?" Jack Hazzard asked that night, standing in the doorway of his parents' bedroom in his pajamas as his mother hung up the phone and began to sob with rage and panic.

"Where the hell have you been?" screamed his mother when Jack's father walked in at 4 A.M., drunk. "Have you been with that whore again?"

"The boy's sleeping. Lower your voice."

"Where the hell have you been, Marcelline?"

"What time is it, anyway?"

"After four!"

"You shouldn't phone me this late, Jack. We're not married."

"You think it would be different if we were?"

"Really, Jack. Goodnight."

"Don't hang u . . ."

"Don't tell me to lower my voice! Jack's been waiting up with me. See! Look, Jackie, your father's drunk."

"You go to sleep now," said his father, escorting Jack to his bedroom, a photograph of Charlie Connerly on the wall, Dad whispering, "Go to sleep now," smelling funny.

"Don't close my door."

"He said don't close his door!" screamed his mother, flinging open her son's door.

"Stop screaming in my house!" screamed his father, slamming shut the door, the light disappearing, all black then in Hazzard's Head, the Depressive there crying.

One time when Jack was twelve Dad didn't come home as he usually did (physically, at least) one Friday night after working late.

"Where's Dad?"

"Daddy's gone away, Jack. He's abandoned us. This toast is burned!"

"I'm scared, Mom."

"Well, if you're scared, then how do you think *I* feel?"

"Goodnight."

"Close my door, dear, the light hurts Mommy's eyes."

Later that night Hazzard heard footsteps on the stairway and then pounding on his mother's bedroom door.

"Marion! Marion, unlock the door. Come on now."

Hazzard stepped into the hallway.

"Hi, Dad."

"Go to bed."

"Are you going to stay now? Mom said you abandoned us."

"I said, go to bed!"

"I'm sorry. Don't close my door!"

"Marion! Marion, I'm going to kick this God damn door down if you don't open it. Marion!"

Peeking timidly into the hallway, Jack Hazzard watched his father kick in the door. Then Dad was standing above Jack's mother, who lay moaning in bed. Dad was examining a container of pills.

"How many did you take, Marion? Wake up! Are you pretending? Did you take all these pills again?"

"What is it, Dad?"

"Jack! Quick! Call the hospital!"

"Which one?"

"Ask for an ambulance. Tell them it's an emergency."

"What's the number?"

"Stop crying. This is an emer . . . never mind. Marion! Wake up!"

"I'm sorry."

"Stop crying!"

"Fuck me, darling. I want to feel you inside of me so much."

"Maybe I'll strangle you first."

"I know you're too scared."

"Maybe a little."

"Choke me while you're inside of me. Kiss me and choke me, darling."

"If you want me to."

"Stop crying, Jack. Look, Mommy's fine now. See. She's walking around. She had a bad stomachache and threw up, and now she's fine. See? Marion? Honey? Tell Jack you're okay now."

When his mother opened her mouth to speak she commenced to vomit, Mr. Hazzard cupping his hands, catching it, saying, "Jesus Christ, Marion!" and leading her back into the bathroom.

"What's wrong with Mom?"

"Jack! Quick! Get a towel."

"A paper one or a regular one?"

"Just any one, damn it. Quit crying!"

"Do you like when I come in your face?"

"Yes, darling. But get a towel."

"The red one or the blue one?"

"Hurry, darling. It's starting to run down my cheek."

"Now you can do what you want to me," Hazzard said.

"I want you to go home now, darling."

When Hazzard's mother was eighteen she worked in a war plant in Kearny, New Jersey, for twenty-five cents an hour. She had to wake at 6 A.M. to catch the bus before walking an additional mile to the plant in order to save a nickel.

"You don't know what it was like, Jackie. You can't imagine what it was like."

"What about my test tomorrow, Mom? I don't understand what 'Y' stands for."

"I don't either, honey. Wait until your father gets home."

"When will he be home?"

"I don't know; he's working late. It's Christmas season and you didn't even offer to help him."

"He didn't ask me to help him."

"He shouldn't have to ask you. You're his son."

"Is he mad?"

"You'll have to ask him that yourself when he gets home."

"I'll call him. I don't want him to be mad."

"You'd better not disturb him now, Jack."

"What's for dinner?"

"I'll get up in a little while and make you something if I have the strength."

"Dad! Listen, Mom's not telling the truth. The reas . . ."

"Jack, I'm exhausted," his father said, climbing the stairs at 10 P.M. during the Christmas season of 1962, when Jack was eleven.

"Just listen a second, okay? See, the reas . . ."

"We'll talk at breakfast, son. Where's your mom?"

"In bed. She got another headache. You want some canned soup I made us?"

"I ate at the store. Goodnight, Jack."

"Wait—listen! Because the reason I got this bad grade Mom's going to tell you about is because . . ."

"Just do your best, son. Goodnight."

"Don't close the door, okay?"

"Calm down and shush now. Your mom's sleeping." His father started into the bedroom, whispering, "And why the heck didn't you shovel the walk? I nearly broke my ass on the snow and ice."

"Listen—I had to do my math, which I don't understand. Then I made soup for me and you because Mom had a headache and . . ."

"Do I have to ask you to do things you should think about on your own? You live here too, you know."

"Are you mad at me for not working at your store because it's Christmas?"

"A little. Now goodnight."

"You would like to order now, please?"

Looking up from the beer, Hazzard told the waiter he was waiting for his wife.

"Yes, yes, very good, sir."

Hazzard lit a cigarette and pulled the Patient's book from his trenchcoat. A clock on the wall indicated 10:35.

> Because the masochistic person cannot possibly stand any distance between himself and the partner, not to speak of separation, he actually feels enslaved. He feels that he has to accept the terms of the partner, no matter what they are. But since he hates his own dependency, resenting it as a humiliation, he is bound to rebel inwardly against any partner, no matter how considerate.
>
> . . . The masochistic person's hostility toward the partner constitutes a constant, unrelieved danger, because he needs the partner and is bound to be afraid of alienating [her].
>
> . . . [Therefore] at any . . . acute rise of hostility anxiety may ensue. But an increase in anxiety increases in turn the need to hang on to the partner. The vicious circle thus operating make a separation increasingly difficult and painful. The conflict inherent in the human relationships of the masochistic person is thus ultimately a conflict between dependency and hostility.
>
> . . . Actually the masochistic person is incapable of love, nor does he believe that the partner or anyone else can love him. What appears under the flag of devotion is actually a sheer clinging to the partner for the sake of allaying anxiety. Hence the precarious nature of this kind of security, and the never-vanishing fear of being deserted. Any friendly gesture on the part of the partner brings reassurance, but any kind of interest

that the partner may have for other people or for [her] own work, any failure to satisfy the permanent hunger for signs of positive interest, may at once conjure up the danger of desertion and thereby engender anxiety.

In short, his terror of wrongdoing simply compels him to feel himself the victim, even when in actual fact he has been the one who failed others or who, through his implicit demands, has imposed upon them. Because feeling victimized thus becomes a protection against his self-hate, it is a strategical position, to be defended vigorously.

"What are you reading, darling?"

When Hazzard looked up, Marcelline Tatia bent down to kiss him, her head hooded in fur. Then she sat down across from him.

"Are you angry with me?" she asked, removing the mink jacket.

Hazzard put away the book. "No."

"Good. How was the reading?"

"Not bad."

"Good." She opened the menu. "I'm starving!"

"Beer?"

"Yes, darling. And then I want the chicken tandoori." She closed the menu and smiled at Hazzard. "Do I look pretty to you?"

Hazzard finished pouring the beer and stared. Her sweater was black cashmere, black liner was drawn around her blue eyes, and her hair, long and luminous, was parted in two folds, hooked behind her ears.

"Beautiful," he told her.

"Kiss me hello nicely then."

She leaned forward, Hazzard kissing her quickly, taking her offered hand.

"You're so bashful in public," she said, putting her foot between his legs beneath the table, and winking.

"Yes, please," the waiter said.

Hazzard ordered for them.

"Thank you, please."

"Cheers!" Hazzard said, thinking of Jill Downs now as he and Marcelline touched glasses and drank.

"Know what?" she said playfully, her tongue moving on her lips.

"What?"

She leaned forward now to whisper, "After dinner I want to go to that sex store and buy toys!"

He felt her foot press again between his legs.

"What kind?" he said, excited initially, but then scared, the Punk and Paranoid clashing.

She told him.

"You're crazy," he said.

"And handcuffs too," she said, her eyes sparkling.

After dinner they walked crosstown along the deserted streets in the direction of The Pink Pussycat. Marcelline held him tightly around the waist and he draped his arm around her shoulder, stroking the fur of her jacket.

"I have a friend," she told him, "who says she burns out a vibrator a month."

"Must be French," he said, cold and tired suddenly, lost and afraid of himself now, remembering Jill Downs and a friendlier time (and a time before that, too, the Patient realized, that was not so friendly).

"How did you know she's French?" Marcelline seemed excited and playful.

"Let's go home to bed," he said.

"Oh, you!" she said. "You're just scared to experiment."

"You're not?" he said, straining for an insouciant tone.

"I'm not scared of anything, darling. I love that about myself. And so do you."

When they reached the sex store, they huddled against the cold and examined the window display of vibrators, dildos, handcuffs and masks.

"Go on," Hazzard said, winking and nodding. "I'll wait for you."

"Very funny!" she said, nudging him with her hip. "But really, darling. Go on. Buy the vibrator and the handcuffs."

"No way, José."

"Oh, Jack. You're so boring sometimes."

He whispered fearfully, "I'm not going in there and asking for a vibrator and handcuffs!"

"You're the man, darling. It's your responsibility."

"Sorry," he said unapologetically.

She leaned close to him and pinched his nose.

"Don't you want to handcuff me, darling . . . and, you know."

Hazzard looked down the street and then back at Marcelline.

"Let's not do this anymore," he said quietly.

"But I want to," she said, not understanding.

He shook his head. "I'm tired."

"Oh! I hate when you're so boring."

She turned and walked away, toward Sixth Avenue. Hazzard trotted after her.

"You're not actually mad?"

"Yes!"

"Why?"

"Because you're no fun! There's a Checker!"

She raised her leather-gloved hand and the cab pulled to the corner. She jumped in and gave the driver her address. Hazzard got in beside her and heard the Son's obsequious and whining tone in the Lover's voice as he said, "Still mad?"

"No!" she cried, suddenly flinging her arms around him and whispering, "Those things were disgusting. I love you so much for respecting me."

Hazzard turned from her in silence and stared out the window of the cab.

Stroking his hair, Marcelline whispered into his ear, "Tomorrow night I want to watch TV and take Quaaludes and fuck."

Hazzard turned back to her. "What's wrong with tonight?"

"I have to go to a disco tonight."

"You're kidding."

"I have to meet some people, darling. So don't start."

"I'm too exhausted to go to a disco."

"Go to bed then."

The Depressive in him didn't have the energy to go on with himself, let alone with her. When the cab stopped at a red light on Thirty-first Street, Hazzard hopped out impulsively. "Goodnight," he said.

"Don't be stupid!"

But the Recluse in him closed the cab door and walked away.

"Don't phone too early, darling!" he heard her call, and the cab moved away, uptown.

EiGHteen

TWICE a week Jack's mother modeled bathing suits or furs in Manhattan. Jack hated Manhattan. He'd visited there twice with his dad, who stopped at wholesale shoe houses to examine the latest lines. The foot models were always happy to see his dad, kissing him on the lips, Dad saying, "Hey, my son's with me, for God's sake!" Jack blushing, burying his head in Dad's hip, sullen and silent, Dad saying, "Go on, Jack, tell Dominique your name."

"Jack."

Mommy was somewhere else modeling bathing suits, not meeting Dad and him for lunch, out with someone else: Manhattan.

When he was alone without her, it was his responsibility to answer the phone and take a message.

"I'd like to speak with Marion."

"My mom's modeling. Who's calling, please?"

"Who's this?"

"This is her son, Jack. I'm supposed to ask who's calling."

"Marion's not home?"

"No, sir. Who's calling, please?"

"You just tell her Al called from Manhattan. You got that? Al."

When he was ten, a man who drove a red Cadillac and had slick black hair would drop in for a drink on those Friday nights when Jack's father was working late at the shoe store. He sat next to Mom on the sofa. She was drinking, too, like a big show-off, laughing all the time, Jack scared and jealous, waiting to hear Daddy's car already on the gravel driveway; he'd show them, yell and punch hard, Jack on the stairway listening, fists closing, jealous and hating, Marcelline out to all hours, "sniffing" and laughing, showing off, no bra.

"When's Dad getting home?" Jack asked, peeking into the living room from his perch on the stairway.

"Soon, honey. Do you know Mr. Craner?"

"Will you help me with my homework now, Mom?"

"It's Friday night, dear. You never do your homework on Friday. Isn't *The Fugitive* on?"

"Yes. Can I watch TV in the living room?"

"Honey, Mr. Craner and I are talking. You may watch in the upstairs den."

"Can I call Dad at the store and see when he's coming home already?"

"Daddy doesn't like to be disturbed when he's working late."

"Can I bring Mike upstairs with me to watch then?"

"I want Mike to stay in the basement."

"Mom, I don't feel so good."

"Then just lie down and nap, honey."

Hazzard pounded up the stairs cursing, then tiptoed down again to his secret perch on the stairs, eavesdropping.

"Jackie?" said his mother. "Is that you, honey? Go upstairs if you don't feel well. I can see your shadow on the wall. Daddy will be home in a little while."

"I'm just getting a stupid cookie!" Slamming cabinets in the kitchen, not wanting a cookie really, going into the basement to hold Mike, crying, talking to the turtles in the tank, too; Mike licking his tears.

"Mom, who's Mr. Craner?"

"Oh, you mean Big Joe. He's a gangster friend of mine."

"Is he a friend of Dad's too?"

"No."

"Does Dad know Al?"

"Al? Al Bornstein?"

"I don't know. He keeps calling you."

"Did he leave a number?"

"No."

"When did he call?"

"Why do you model bathing suits in Manhattan?"

"To make money, dear."

"You said Dad was rich."

"When did Al call, honey?"

The beds in his parents' bedroom were connected by a gold hook and eye. When his mother made the beds she would listen on the radio to "Make-Believe Ballroom," hosted by William B. Williams (Willie B!). On days when Hazzard remained home from school with a cold he would listen to her dancing and singing to the music while he read a Hardy Boys book which she had brought him at Klein's department store, along with a present, such as a new shirt, a map of a foreign country, or athletic equipment such as a ball or a bat.

"Thanks. Thanks!"

"I hope you get well now, Jackie."

"I will."

"The dog's been on the bed, hasn't he?"

"I'm sorry."

"Where is he now?"

"In the closet, hiding."

"Well, I guess it won't hurt if he stays in the room," opening the closet and patting Mike, Jack crying, "Thanks, Mom. Thanks!"

"Just not on the bed."

"I promise."

If he wanted one sports jacket she bought him two; if two pair of pants, three. When he went to camp, she sewed his name in all his clothing. She cooked delicious food. When he had a cold, she held his hand, changed his bed, held his juice glass so he could drink with his head still on the pillow, cooled the soup in the spoon by blowing on it first before he sipped.

"Good?"

"Great!"

"Want more of Mommy's soup?"

"Thanks, Mom. Your soup's great!"

But she wrecked his room, punished him frequently and arbitrarily, hit him with wooden hangers and scolded him for his dirty underwear (because it itched so he scratched, not knowing that she'd look and shame him), and lied to his father about him. He never knew when she would become mean and strange, Mommy like two different people, Jackie's fear of her diffuse and constant, her finger always on the trigger, Jack waiting and afraid, hiding with Mike.

"Want to dance, Jackie?" his mother asked the eleven-year-old Hazzard, as she kicked her legs, panting before the mirror in her bedroom, moving to the music of "Make-Believe Ballroom."

"No."

"Come on. I'll teach you."

"Dad said I should try to go to the park and play hoops."

Mommy dancing, panting, watching herself in the mirror, saying breathlessly, "Oh, come on and dance. *We won't tell him.*"

She taught Hazzard and his friends how to dance. Three of his sixth-grade friends would come to his house on Monday afternoons and Jack's mother would teach them how to fox-trot, jitterbug, twist and charleston. The boys were all members of Jack's Boy Scout troop, of which Mrs. Hazzard was the den mother.

"Your mom sure is a great dancer, Jack," said his friend Joe, who, along with Blaine and Doyle, drank Yoo-Hoos in the kitchen after their lessons.

"She can sing, too," Jack said proudly.

"I wish my mom was nice like yours."

"She buys me books. Want to see my collection?" (which she would throw out the week after Jack moved away to college).

Jack all proud showing them the books and the picture of his mom he kept on his night table (and which he would take away with him to college).

"Your mom sure is pretty. Lucky stiff!"

"She lets me zip up her dress. I've seen her in her girdle and stuff. You ever seen your mom like that?"

"Are you nuts?"

"Well, I watch my mom before she goes to parties."

"Lucky stiff."

"My dad's penis is too big for her."

"What?"

"Come on, honey, dance with Mommy!"

"Dance with Dad!"

"That old fart!"

But sometimes she was happy. Sometimes Mom and Dad danced. Jack would watch them broodingly, warily, waiting for the fight to start, the shouting, Daddy's hands in his pockets, Mommy yelling again about Jack's shoes left in the hallway, the God damn dog, crying in his room, hurt and hiding, his room smaller each year he got bigger. But sometimes she was happy, Mom and Dad dancing, Jack coming out of his head, the world not so bad, nice now, going in the car with Mom when he was little, waiting with her in the butcher shop for the lamb chops she was buying, sawdust on the floor, Mommy asking the butcher to show Jackie the chops because she was buying them special for him, calling them Jackie lamb chops, holding her hand, Mommy pretty and nice too now. The bakery next door, across the street Daddy's shoe store, going out to lunch, all three of them, Mommy and Daddy holding hands sometimes, kissing on the lips, Jack watching, Daddy picking him up, hugging him, Jack holding on, Daddy's after-shave nice, wanting to stay, Mommy and Daddy happy, the chops and cookies in a bag for supper, Mike waiting in the car, Mommy letting him come along that day, Jack wishing it could always be nice like this, no yelling, no fear, no hating, not hiding in his head alone, all hurt, scared after Mommy went crazy yelling and throwing, hitting and lying, Daddy lonely and sad and mean, Jack only acting, dead like the lamb.

Nineteen

I T was nearly 1 A.M. when Hazzard reached home. He poured himself a glass of Paddy's Irish whiskey and lay on the living-room rug before the fireplace, the Lover, Son, Punk and Paranoid united now in their conviction that Marcelline was running around tonight, playing him for the fool. Sipping the drink, staring into the ashes of the fireplace, the Patient wondered why Hazzard countenanced such behavior, his own as well as hers. "What's your investment in this morbid dependency?" he asked the Lover. "What's the difference," quipped the Writer defensively. "It's a story, isn't it?" "But there's a rather curious omission to your story," the Patient said to the Writer. "By which I mean, given all the characters you've created for him, I can't understand why there's not the *Man* in Hazzard's Head. Could you explain that to the Lover?"

Hazzard poured himself another drink. The Depressive wanted to go to bed, but the Patient wanted an answer, Hazzard sitting now at the kitchen table with his book.

The sexuality which Freud describes is unmistakably that sexual obsession which shows itself whenever a patient has reached the point where he needs to be forced or tempted out of a wrong attitude or situation. It is an overemphasized sexuality piled up behind a dam; and it shrinks to normal proportions as soon as the way to development is opened. It is being caught in the old resentments against the parents and relations and in the boring emotional tangles of the family situation which most often brings about the damming-up of the energies of life. And it is this stoppage which shows itself unfailingly in the kind of sexuality which is called "infantile."

"When I was engaged to your mother I used to screw this actress named Karen," his father told him. "Unfortunately, you see, my penis scared your mother."

"I know," Jack said. "It was too big for her. Also, she hated when you stuck your tongue in her mouth."

"How did you know that?"

"And you wanted to have relations with her on Sunday after playing tennis but she wouldn't brush her teeth."

"How did you know that?" repeated his father.

"Because she tells me everything just like you do."

"Hardly everything," his father said, winking.

With the infallibility of a sleepwalker, the analysand seeks out those who, like his parents (though for different reasons), certainly cannot understand him. Through his compulsive need to repeat, he will try to make himself understandable to precisely these people—trying to make possible what cannot be.... The fascination of such tormenting relationships is part of the compulsion constantly to reenact one's earliest disappointments with the parents.

Hazzard lit a cigarette and stared into the amber depths of his drink. "Hey," said the Paranoid, "I'm not the problem here. Marcelline Tatia's to blame." "The problem here," the Teacher told the Patient, "inheres in identifying your real self with these false selves." "Pick a face, any face!" the Actor told the Boy, shuffling his postures as if they were playing cards. "You mean," said the Boy, "we're just a face created to face other faces?" "What you are," said the Writer impatiently, "is a character of my imagination." "A man's character is his fate," the Teacher recited to the Son. "A man becomes his thinking." "So I bought a ticket to my own show," said the Actor contentiously, "and sold tickets to the others. They don't know the difference between truth and illusion—maybe there isn't one!" "I *guess* I'm only playing," said the Boy, frowning, trying to understand Hazzard's Head. "Why play in the dark," said the Teacher, "when you can play in the Light?" "What's the Light?" asked the Son nervously. "The Light is the Truth that Liberates," said the Teacher, "while the Dark is the Falsehood that Enslaves." "I don't like the light," the Punk responded. "It hurts my eyes when I fuck. Besides," he told the Boy, "if you play with yourself in the light the Mother will catch you!" "But he *is* caught," said the Patient. "Caught in the Depressive's web of contradictory needs and emotions." "You mean I'm the spider and also the fly?" said the Boy. "It's not my fault!" said the Paranoid, pointing to the Son and shouting, "He's the one who did this to us! He's the one who created all of us to protect him from his true feelings for the Mother and the Father." "The *Man?*" the Patient again asked the Writer. "Why's there no Man in Hazzard's Head?" "That's precisely whom I'm trying to liberate," the Teacher said.

The telephone rang.

Hazzard glanced at his wristwatch: 2:33 A.M.

He stood, the Paranoid letting the phone ring twice more before the Lover picked up, the Actor cautious.

"Yes?"

"I miss you, darling."

Hazzard remained silent, staring out the living-room window to the deserted avenue, where pieces of newsprint sailed in circles as the Recluse counted six yellow cabs speeding south.

"I want to come over now, darling. Hello?"

Hazzard hung up, the Recluse protecting the Paranoid.

"What the hell did you do that for?" said the Lover. "I'm tired," said the Depressive. "I need sleep." "Now she'll probably fuck some other guy," said the Paranoid. "I'm sick of you pussies," said the Punk, "and I'm sick of that bitch, too." "Let go of her already," said the Patient, the Boy running to the Mother, taking her hand, clinging. "No!" said the Boy, the Son adding impulsively, "I like being angry." I like fighting with ourselves." "It comforts me," said the Lover. "It makes me feel right at home."

A panic suddenly ascended in Hazzard with the Patient's epiphany that the Lover's compulsive clinging to Marcelline was informed by a much more fundamental fear of letting go of nearly all the inhabitants of his head that had been created by the Son and Boy to hold on to the Mother and the Father in fear and hurt and rage. Letting go of Marcelline would require the arrested Son and Boy to relinquish control of Hazzard to the Man. "And the rest of us?" inquired the Paranoid. "Might not such a change in Hazzard's Head require the death of us?"

The phone rang again.

"Don't!" said the Recluse and Paranoid in chorus. "Fuck you!" said the Punk, sidekick and alter ego of the Son, the Lover picking up at once.

"I know I'm bad, darling. Are you mad at me?"

"I guess," Hazzard said, weak now with the fear of renouncing his old concepts of himself, which informed his obsession for Marcelline Tatia.

"Do you want to see me tonight? Because I've been sniffing coke and miss you so much right now."

Hazzard could hear disco music pounding like a migraine headache in the background.

"Where are you?"

"Close by."

Hazzard noted his reflection floating in the blackened window before him. Why should he let go of her if it would entail letting go of the very personality he'd structured long ago to save himself from tyrannies that had threatened to crush the Son and the Boy? "Because," the Depressive said, "it hurts too much now." "Because this personality of ours is a house of cards!" interjected the actor, sick of the same old act. "That's just too God damn bad about you!" hollered the Mother, hitting the Boy repeatedly over the head with her handbag.

"Do you admit you were bad?" the regressive Son had the obsessive Lover ask for Hazzard.

"M-hm," Marcelline said. "But only because I know you love that about me."

"I don't."

She was speaking to someone else now—laughing.

"Listen," Hazzard said. "I'm tired . . ."

"I'm coming over," she said hurriedly.

"Maybe tomorrow."

"Don't you want to tie me up for being bad?"

The Punk winked at the Depressive in Hazzard's Head. "Go for it!" he told the Actor.

"Chop chop!" Hazzard surrendered cynically, hanging up with a hateful smirk.

Seated on the living-room sofa, the Patient read to keep

Hazzard distracted from the greater distraction of Marcelline Tatia. But by 3:30 A.M. he couldn't keep his eyes open. The Lover demanded that Hazzard phone Marcelline's apartment. The answering machine announced: "I'm not available for the moment. Please leave your name and number and I'll return your call as soon as possible. Have a nice day."

With the help of ten milligrams of the Patient's Valium, all thirteen of Hazzard slid into a semicomatose sleep, the Punk telling the narcotized Lover right before losing consciousness, "Next time I get my hands on her, she's dead meat. You dig?"

Part Three

Twenty

THE alarm signaled at 8:30 A.M. and the Writer, hung over, commanded Hazzard to commence his work.

"It's getting late," the Father told the Son, who screamed to the Writer, "Hurry up already! I don't want to be punished with anxiety by the Father." "I'm afraid," the Mother said, tying her apron in place and feeling put upon, "that Jackie's going to need a big pot of coffee this morning."

Anxious, Hazzard stood beneath the shower's cascade of hot water until it lost its heat. Calmer now, and wrapped in his bathrobe, he watched the coffee percolating on the stove top.

"What a stupid life," said the Depressive. "Writing books, no one ever around, never any fun, completely anonymous, poor to boot!" "You've gotten exactly what you deserve," said the Father. "Hey, my good man," said the Punk, "don't put me down. Put down the Lover for letting the bitch yank him around by his little dick." "If Dad couldn't put down

Mom," said the Son, "how can I put down Marcelline?"
"Watch!" exclaimed the Punk, scratching his cock.

As Hazzard poured himself a cup of coffee, a knock
sounded at the door.

"Don't answer it," entreated the Recluse, the Paranoid
tiptoeing to the door nonetheless to peek through the peep-
hole.

"I hear you, darling. Open up!"

"What do you want?" Hazzard said.

"I want to talk with you."

"How did you get in? Where the hell have you been?"

"Open the door and I'll explain."

The Actor rehearsed a beleaguered and disaffected posture before allowing the Lover to open the door for Hazzard.
The Father, meanwhile, backed away, hands thrust in his
pockets.

Marcelline entered and looked Hazzard up and down as
he stood silently sipping coffee before her in his robe, sweatsocks and sunglasses.

"You look cute," she said, her voice raspy with exhaustion. "Coffee for me too?"

She smelled of cigarette smoke and her face needed washing, her makeup smeared and cracking.

"Haven't you been to bed?"

"Of course not."

She walked into the kitchen and poured herself a cup of
coffee.

"Doing coke, have we?" Hazzard said.

"What do you think?"

"From the edge in the voice I'd say shame on you, my
dear." He wagged his finger disapprovingly at her.

"Don't start with me. I met some people."

"I'd put a cork up the asshole of that tone real quick," Hazzard said, the Punk just waiting, pushing his way to the front of the line in Hazzard's Head.

"Oh! I don't care about my tone. I came by to tell you I'm leaving town again, not to fight with you again."

"When are you leaving?"

"Now look at you! So scared and worried, like a child."

"When?"

"Three days. That's why I didn't come by last night. I met some people. They want me to work with them in Saint Bart."

"On what?"

"Parties."

"Parties?"

"Parties?" Marcelline mimicked hatefully.

The Writer said for Hazzard now, "These incredible canards of yours only inspire incredulity, my dear."

"Talk so I can understand."

"I'm sick of your bullshit."

"Don't be so mean and stupid. I'm tired."

"Why the fuck didn't you phone me?"

"I forgot. Look, darling, for once just accept our affair for what it's good for."

"What's it good for?"

"Sex."

"I'm afraid," Hazzard said unpleasantly and emphatically, "that the fucking I get is not worth the fucking I get. So get out."

"You expect too much from me."

"Just decency."

"It's not like we're married, Jack. We're only lovers. It could be nice."

"Well, since it's over now, get out."

"Darling, some people live their entire life and never have what we have in bed."

"I can't isolate what we have in bed from what we don't have out of bed."

"Try."

"I did!"

Suddenly she smiled, then began to laugh, putting her hand to her mouth and staring into Hazzard's furious eyes.

"What the hell's so funny?"

She laughed again. "I just realized what it is about us, darling. I'm the man and you're the woman. It's like you're my unhappy wife!"

Setting down her coffee cup on the kitchen table, Marcelline buttoned up her fur coat and blew Hazzard a kiss.

"All right then, darling. It's finished. I'm not going to play your husband any more. Ciao!"

Twenty-one

"**W**HAT happened then?" Dr. Roth asked that afternoon.

"She said she was finished playing my husband and left."

"How did you feel?"

"I felt like chucking her out the window."

"Because she called you 'her unhappy wife,' or because she wouldn't play your husband?"

Hazzard closed his eyes and sighed. "Then you agree with her?"

"About what?"

"About a sexual role reversal."

"Well," Roth interposed calmly, "was there one?"

"What do you think?"

"By your stridency I think you feel Marcelline articulated a very strong fear of yours."

"I'm not my mother, Doctor!"

"Why do you mention your mother?"

"She's the unhappy wife, not me."

"You'd prefer to be the unhappy husband, you mean?"

"Why do you mention my father?" Hazzard said mordantly.

"The unhappy son then?" Roth said, undaunted.

"I thought we were talking about Marcelline and me."

"We are, ostensibly."

"Ostensibly?"

Roth's averted eyes suggested impatience. "Perhaps," he said, clearing his throat, "it's safer for you, with Marcelline, to play the unhappy wife than to play the unhappy husband? Or is it merely a reenactment of the good and unhappy son that we're talking about?"

"Frankly, I haven't the slightest idea what you're talking about."

"Well," Roth said, with an exaggerrated sense of concentration, "who would you say you are more afraid of? Mom or Dad?"

"Mom," Hazzard answered.

"I assume, then, that this explains why you frequently talk as much as a woman?"

"I'm afraid, if you want to provoke me," Hazzard responded, "you'll have to be far more subtle."

"About what? That I question whether you're attracted to girls? That I think you're more afraid of your mother than even your father was?"

"I refuse to participate in this crap."

"Really? But then why do you remain with someone like Marcelline when she's no less dedicated to emasculating you than Mom and Dad were?"

"Who knows?"

"You."

"I'll think about it over the weekend," Hazzard replied vacantly.

"Is it really easier to punish yourself with Marcelline than acknowledge the terrible, unconscious mistake your parents committed?"

"Perhaps," Hazzard answered anxiously, his face wan and averted.

"But tell me, Jack—how much longer are you going to punish yourself for fear of your rage at your father's unhappy wife?"

Hazzard noted the clock on the mantel above the fireplace.

"I'm afraid we're out of time, Doctor."

Roth ignored Hazzard's hostile inflection. "Why not distance yourself from Marcelline until she's left town?"

"Why not *not* tell me what to do?"

"Tell me about your plans for the weekend."

"Haven't any."

"New Year's weekend and no plans?"

"I'd planned on hanging out with Marcelline."

"Planning on drinking?"

"I never plan on it."

Hazzard stood and shook Roth's hand.

"Thanks so much for the help, Doctor. I'll see you next year."

"Don't hesitate," Roth offered when Hazzard reached the door, "to contact me by phone if the need arises."

Traversing the park in the December twilight, Hazzard experienced an ungovernable paroxysm of rage. He could feel the Punk pressing for command now in order to focus this fury into a coherent strategy of action. For Friday afternoon could be such a confusing time for the Punk, especially now when the old year was drawing to a close and circumstances demanded a decision on what to do next. Fortunately, the Punk's special virtuosity was his capacity to marshal the anxiety of Hazzard's psychic turmoil toward simple acts of vengeful indignation. In a crisis such as this, the Punk could be relied upon to blame and then assault the culpable object or objects that the Paranoid considered responsible for Hazzard's dilemma.

Of course, if no immediate object of blame came to mind, then the Punk had little compunction about resorting to the adventure of punishing the Depressive in Hazzard by way of abusing alcohol or drugs. For surely, the Punk reasoned now, a man needed adventure to revivify the psyche from the debilitations of daily routine. Oh, perhaps unhappy wives could countenance the repressions of domestic monotony, but a man—at least one who wasn't a pussy—required adventure.

Yet how strange, the Punk mused, that the need for adventure so frequently translated into hunting for broads—their bush being the last wilderness left in the leveled urban landscape. Because, really now, without that wild, deep and dark continent of the cunt, what remained to the adventurer but shopping? And Davey *Cockett,* king of the Punk's wild frontier, didn't dig shopping on Friday afternoons. No, Big Davey *Cockett* was wild for that last wilderness.

Hazzard found himself wandering *west* to check out the All-State Café. Inside, logs burned brightly in the fireplace as *Talking Heads* played on the jukebox. He sat at the bar next to the Punk's favorite waitress, a slinky little number in tight designer jeans and a baggy sweater scalloped at the throat.

Hazzard ordered a boilermaker from Charles.

"Heaven Hill?"

"Let's be elegant tonight, Charles. Paddy's."

Charles set down the shot and chaser. "So?"

"So what?"

"Getting any?"

"No complaints."

"You don't look like you got no complaints."

"Fuck you, too. Cheers!"

Hazzard killed the shot and, sipping his beer, opened a book.

"Hey," Charles said, "I'm lonely. Talk to me."

Hazzard raised his eyes from the book to the cigarette smoke circling Charles, who wiped the bar's varnished surface and poured Hazzard another set.

"Tell me about them little hairs you got stuck between your teeth, Jack."

"No locker-room report today," Hazzard answered, and, sliding a five on the bar, moved away to a table, where the Patient resumed his reading.

> Suffering is unconsciously put into the service of asserting claims, which not only checks the incentive to overcome it but also leads to inadvertent exaggerations of suffering. This does not mean that his suffering is merely "put on" for demonstrative purposes. It affects him in a much deeper way because he must primarily prove to himself, to his own satisfaction, that he is entitled to the fulfillment of his needs. He must feel that his suffering is so exceptional and so excessive that it entitles him to help. In other words this process makes a person actually feel his suffering more intensely than he would without its having acquired an unconscious strategic value.
>
> Suffering thus acquires another function: that of absorbing rage.

Looking for the waitress now, the Punk impatient for his next Paddy's, Hazzard heard his heart begin to accelerate with anger. The Paranoid sensed something developing, something ungovernable surfacing with the slow slide of the brain into that Reptilian realm of Hazzard's psyche that frightened all thirteen of him now, even the Punk, whose function was essentially defensive, but who was planning from necessity to *strike out,* a smile playing on Hazzard's face, snickering to himself, the Patient perceived now as an obstacle, his faith in the melioristic power of understanding a bloody joke to the Actor.

Hazzard gestured to the waitress, who approached now, all legs and crotch, sleazy God damn thing, which is the way the Punk, in fearing and hating them, preferred them.

"What's your name anyway?"

"I can't talk now."

"You just did."

"What'll it be?"

"You working late tonight?"

"Get your own drink, okay?"

Turning away in umbrage from him, her ass retreating so superciliously, Hazzard could not surpress an impulse to help her along with the Punk's well-worn cowboy boot.

Charles approached, hands behind his back.

"Don't bust her chops."

"Don't bust mine."

"Hey, I'm *telling* you."

"You don't tell me anything."

"What the fuck is this tonight?"

"I want a God damn drink, Charles!"

"You can't ask nice?"

Charles brought his hands from behind his back, holding the Paddy's, and poured until the amber-colored medicine quavered on the rim of the shot glass.

"Thank you, Charles."

"Act like an asshole sometimes."

"One more," Hazzard said, reaching the shot glass toward the bottle.

"No trouble, Jack, okay?"

"No trouble."

"Order at the bar, okay?"

"Okay."

"Relax."

"You relax."

"Fuck you, Jack."

"Leave the bottle, Charles."

"Can't."

"I'll leave it under the table like last time."

"Just be careful."

The Punk in Hazzard handed the scumbag a ten-spot.

"For you, Charles. Your kindness."

The pernicious character of neurotic pride lies in the combination of its being vitally important to the individual and at the same time rendering him extremely vulnerable. This situation creates tensions, which, because of their frequency and intensity, are so unbearable that they call for remedies: *automatic endeavors to restore pride when it is hurt and to avoid injuries when it is endangered.*

The need to save face is urgent, and there is more than one way of effecting it. As a matter of fact, there are so many different ways, gross and subtle, that I must restrict my presentation to the more frequent and important ones. The most effective and, it seems, almost ubiquitous one is interlinked with the impulse to take revenge for what is felt as humiliation. We discussed it as a reaction of hostility to the pain and the danger involved in a hurt pride. But the vindictiveness may in addition be a means toward self-vindication. It involves the belief that by getting back at the offender one's own pride will be restored. This belief is based on the feeling that the offender, by his very power to hurt our pride, has put himself above us and has defeated us. By our taking revenge and hurting him more than he did us, the situation will be reversed. We will be triumphant and will have defeated him. The aim of the neurotic vindictive revenge is not "getting even" but triumphing by hitting back harder. Nothing short of triumph *can* restore the imaginary grandeur in which pride is invested. It is this very capacity to restore pride that gives neurotic vindictiveness its incredible tenacity and accounts for its compulsive character.

Hazzard knocked back two more for good luck and stuffed the Patient's book into his pocket, the Writer stumbling slightly as Hazzard stood, the whiskey working now, Hazzard needing air to steady down, so waving bye-bye to Charles before floating into the nasty night, raw from the river, the Punk's God damn nerves raw from wondering just where the fuck she'd been all last night anyway.

"Let's find out!" the Paranoid suggested, and thus the Lover dropped a quarter into the public phone before dialing Marcelline's number.

Hazzard listened to the ringing while snapping noose-shaped smoke rings into the sky. "Where there's smoke," said the Punk, "there's fire."

"Hello?"

Hazzard smiled at the sound of her voice, his heart pounding as a subway train roared by below, the ground rumbling, the stink of the subterranean rising to his nostrils.

He sneezed.

"Hello?"

"I'm in the neighborhood," he heard himself saying, sniffling, using the back of his hand.

"Of course you're in the neighborhood, darling. You live in the neighborhood."

"You busy?"

"I'm going out soon."

"Well, I'll just come over sooner."

"I knew you'd call me!"

Hazzard could hear music playing in the background and pictured now for some reason the wall of windows in her living room, the cityscape seen from the forty-second floor there reminding him of a mortuary.

Hazzard cleared his throat for the Actor. "I called because I know that you're leaving soon, and naturally, being your friend now, I want to say goodbye."

The Actor was calm, the Punk eying the cowboy boots on the cement, wet with slush, even the Depressive slightly thrilled at the prospect of sticking it to her instead of to Hazzard himself after all these years, the Paranoid figuring maybe she did deserve it, a good ass-kicking, that is, for yanking him around rather unconscionably for over a year now, as if he were some stupid plaything for her amusement, as if the Lover were no better than the Boy or the Son, those abject monkeys-in-the-middle between the Mother and the Father.

"I want to be your friend, Jack," she said. "Do you really want to be my friend?"

"I'll be right over," Hazzard said. "Ciao, darling."

It was the Punk, finally, who persuaded the Actor to pick up the half pint of Jack Daniel's at the liquor store. Jackie D! That the whiskey didn't go down smoothly mattered less than that it went down fast, because, you know, in general, things hadn't gone down smoothly for Hazzard for a long time now, but maybe he should have done something about that a lot sooner, but, no, he had just let things go until all at once, it seemed, it had to come up, volcanic and vicious now, the Punk trying to explain for years how Hazzard had been taken advantage of without defending himself. Oh, yes, he'd been very much of a pussy in the Punk's opinion, a little mommy's boy with his hands in his pockets like his old man all those years, never doing a God damn thing about a whole lot of abuse. What did she think, this little Italian bitch, that he'd let her get away with calling him 'her unhappy wife' like she was his father or something, calling him Shirley because he wore his hair long to hide his birthmark until that bastard pimp of a barber had cut it off like Marcelline was trying to do to his balls, his mother just like her always on his case even about his underpants being dirty like she had a right to go snooping in the hamper, or his shoes never in the right slots in the shoe bag, wrecking his room for that and then dancing before the mirror to "Make-Believe Ballroom," how he'd made believe a million times of going in there and wrecking her stuff as she did his like he wasn't even a human being with a heart and mind, trying to explain that to Dad all those years but, no, Dad was always too tired to even listen as if Jack didn't even matter as a person.

Hazzard hoped somebody would open their big fucking mouth when he hurled the empty half pint of Jack Daniel's into the avenue, but the bus accelerating drowned out the crash.

Hazzard crossed the avenue talking to himself, his hands pantomiming a boxer's, and then he entered the lobby of Marcelline's building.

The cigarette he lit there steadied him down, his nerves a little less close to kicking out now.

"Evening, Mr. Hazzard."

Hazzard nodded to the doorman, the Actor smooth, eyes hidden behind the Recluse's prescription sunglasses, walking calmly to the elevator, hearing the doorman announcing him on the house phone to Marcelline Tatia, who thought no doubt that she was just going away the first of the week without the Actor having his big scene.

Stepping into the elevator, Hazzard noted his head's reflection, deformed and grotesque, in the convex security mirror. He saluted in recognition.

"My number one man!" the Punk said in Hazzard's Head.

Then he was ascending with a simple push of a button to the top of the building to her rich girl's apartment for which her erstwhile boyfriend who'd queered up on her was paying the rent. So what did Marcelline think? That just because she was so high up she was above it all?

The penthouse hallway smelled now of pot roast like Grandma's apartment building for all those years when he had to get dressed up like a goody two-shoes never saying anything in protest, just putting up with being pushed around, what'd they all think, he was a doormat they could wipe their filthy shoes on forever and ever?

He rang the doorbell and put his ear to the door. He could hear her blabbing away on the phone, always making him wait, making him ring it again and again now, always with her cute little castrating way of humiliating him like that, him: her unhappy wife!

She let him in after taking her own sweet time about it with the locks. He entered, eyes averted, and walked past her into the living room, where he opened his black wool coat, leaving his hands in his pockets, eyes addressing the wall of windows as he heard the bolts behind him relock and the chain slide in place.

He turned now to see her standing before him in a sheer white blouse, no bra underneath, lacy white skirt, her red high heels matching the thick red belt adorned with silver at her cute little waist, the lipstick and nail polish red too. Well, well! But what was really too bad about it all, too fucking bad, was that he liked her a lot but she had to make a fool of him for liking her, treating her pretty good considering, taking her for dinner and to the movies and theater, not cheating on her, but no, that wasn't enough, never good enough for her, making him feel the fool by running around to all hours of the morning after saying she loved him.

Then again, here she was now, before him exclusively maybe for the last time, never seeing her look so pretty to be perfectly honest about it, her hair long and so fussed-over-sweeping tonight, the black eyeliner sexy, but not for him anymore, no, just put on tonight to make him jealous—except they were going to be friends, which was really a laugh without, oddly, being at all funny.

"No friendly kiss?" she said.

"No friendly drink, he replies," Hazzard said.

"Help yourself, darling. I have to finish packing."

"Before you go out?"

"I told you I was going out, darling."

He watched her go into the bedroom.

"Packing for your trip to Saint Bart?" he called.

"You got it, Charlie."

Even with his sunglasses the fluorescent lighting in the kitchen hurt his eyes. But he felt good now in his resolution. He smiled at his hands before pouring the vodka, Dad showing him how to defend himself some day just in case, how to hit and move, hands good for something more than playing pocket pool.

Then he noticed a red pocketbook on the sink ledge and rummaged secretly through it, discovering a silver cigarette case containing a dozen meticulously rolled joints, which was most curious indeed, Mr. Watson, as Ms. Tatia didn't know

how to roll joints. And well, well. Would you look at this,
Dr. Holmes, her diaphragm in its cute blue case in the pocketbook which matched her sexy high heels and belt.

"Checkmate!" Hazzard said out loud, but to himself: her
unhappy wife!

He carried the drink carefully into the bedroom to find
pretty Miss Marcelline zipping up two large suitcases, her
back to him, her legs, so lithe and lovely, visible even beneath the skirt, the panties visible too, so he just figured there
wasn't really much to lose now, nothing more than the little
self-respect and self-protection he'd garnered by way of an
intransigent reclusion from people who always shoved it up
his ass like his mother with her enema mania when he was
too little to protect himself and said his stomach hurt.

There were flowers, red roses, in a vase on the night table
beside her bed.

"Who sent you the flowers?" Hazzard said, sipping the
Absolut.

"A friend."

"The one with whom you're going to Saint Bart?"

"That's none of your business now, Jack. We're just
friends."

What surprised him about the beginning of the end was
the way in which he so swiftly and easily picked her up and
pinned her against the wall, his right forearm against her
throat, the poor petite thing unable to breathe now.

"Sorry," he said, feigning confusion, "but I missed that
last little bit. Mind repeating it?"

He thought he heard her say "Stop."

"Stop? You say you want me to stop?"

She nodded.

"All right then, darling," he said softly, stepping away and
releasing her.

"Are you crazy or what?" she gasped.

Something was wrong with her voice, so raspy and weak, and her hand was holding her neck, as if perhaps all that "sniffing" had irritated the glands of her throat.

Hazzard frowned now, closing one eye in consternation, hands thrust in his pockets.

"Did I give you permission to talk? I mean, did I say . . . you know, *say* you could talk?"

"You are bizarre and I hate you. Get out!"

He blinked for a moment, laughing softly in his throat, before smashing her with his open hand, the way his mother had done it to him; and then he watched her crash into the night table and knock over the roses.

Clean up this room!

He kicked the spinning vase into the wall and watched it ricochet into the hallway. Then he stood with his arms folded before his chest and observed Marcelline, her head bowed, crying now on her knees, the dress and shoes wet from the flower water.

"Oh, come on now," Hazzard said skeptically. "We're a big girl. Let's not be a crybaby!"

He yanked her to her feet by her hair before ripping off her blouse and pushing her onto the bed, where she tried, pathetically, really, to cover her nakedness with a pillow.

"That's against the rules!" Hazzard said, yanking away the pillow before ripping off her skirt, the belt staying on above the little white panties, so that he found himself excited by the helplessness of her in the red heels and belt, the little panties showing the hairs of her cunt.

Now look at her! Sobbing on the bed with her hand thrust in her mouth, her legs pulled into her now for protection, but no, oh, no! she wasn't fooling him none, appealing to his pity, because Jack Daniel had no pity tonight.

"God, I'm bored," he said. "Are you bored, darling? Shall we try something more exciting than watching you play crybaby?"

He saw himself now in the mirrored headboard bolted to the wall behind Marcelline's bed. "I've got an idea," he told the reflection, and he began to pace, hands held behind his back as if he were ice-skating.

"Listen up, darling," he said, annoyed now by her sobbing, the Actor in him knowing a performance when he saw one. "Listen up and try to guess why you are in very serious danger. Can you guess, do you think? Well, at least try. Go on, take a wild guess."

He waited, watching her, listening to her sobbing, pretending she was traumatized by a little smash in the face.

"All right, all right," Hazzard said, disgusted. "I'll tell you already, for Christ's sake."

He glanced again at his reflection in the mirror.

"The reason why you're in danger, my darling, is because you live forty-two floors above the surface of the earth and you don't know how to fly!"

The phone rang.

"I'll get it," Hazzard said, and in one movement ripped the phone from its wall socket and hurled it into the open clothes closet.

"I'm sure he'll call you back."

When he went to grab her, she responded by screaming, so he really had no recourse but to press his weight fully against her and, wrapping his arm around her head, squeeze down cruelly. That shut her up fast, like his father never could do all those years to his damn mother who thought she wore the pants in the family: his unhappy wife!

Now with her head locked in his arm, he dragged her from the bedroom and through the living room, stopping at the wall of windows, where he had to struggle momentarily with the lock of the middle encasement with his left hand. When he'd opened the widest window, the wind wafted in, smelling of the foul river which he could see glittering blackly far far below and to the west.

He thought he heard her say "Please!" but it could have been the Boy's voice in his head. Then he thought he heard her say "Don't!" but maybe that was the Lover's voice.

My, my, how strong the wind blew when you were above it all; and how strong it made him feel now as he forced her head out the window to view the city as only the wealthy could afford to view it.

What he did when her belly lay on the window ledge was to slam the window closed on the fancy red belt enwrapping her waist, so that her ass and legs were all that remained to behold of her inside the apartment, the rest of her free as a bird in flight—almost! He was surprised, truly so, not to hear her screaming; but then she didn't even thrash her legs when he ripped off her lacy panties and massaged her high and mighty ass, Mommy always so worried her tushie was too big in her Saturday night party dress, asking Jackie how it looked, while his father read the paper downstairs, the dog whining in the basement, when all Jack wanted really was to be left alone with Mike in his room to watch *The Fugitive,* but that was asking for the God damn impossible—like asking Marcelline to come to his reading—like trying to get his five fingers into her ass now.

She was vomiting. He could hear her retching. And her legs were moving now, awfully good legs, even the back of her thighs still firm for a woman eight years older than he, her ass awfully good too so that another possibility occurred to him as he lowered his zipper and withdrew himself, rubbing his cock now along her legs, his fingers poking around just to remind her who was wearing the pants here.

A helicopter whirred past. Just in case, Hazzard brought down the venetian blind, which settled and gathered at her belted waist as he slowly spread her legs, working his hips between her thighs, her ass hot to his hands and hard cock as she called it, the closed window holding her steady, stroking himself up and down, amazed at how wet she was and at how easily he entered her, amazed at how he climaxed nearly at once, his head buried now in revulsion in the venetian blind.

"Show's over," Hazzard heard himself thinking, the Punk raising his hands in victory (that left the others vanquished).

What Hazzard did at once was drag Marcelline into the apartment, whereupon she collapsed at his feet.

Something, he now noticed, was wrong with her breathing; her entire body was heaving, and from her mouth, open and dirty with vomit, issued a horrible rasp, as if she were choking. Yet he left her to lie limply below him, looking down at his cock limply hanging from his pants, eclipsing her until he absently zipped himself up and, lifting her carefully, carried her into the bedroom.

The Mother in him went at once to the bathroom, soaked a facecloth with cool water and returned to the bed to wipe Marcelline's mouth and nostrils. The sunken crescents beneath her closed eyes were livid against the pallor of her small face, but she was breathing more regularly now. Sitting beside her and waiting, he was careful not to touch her. He smoked a cigarette, then another, waiting to make sure she'd survive, as he was afraid he would, to remember this—his longed for *resolution*.

At the very moment he thought she'd fallen asleep, he discovered her staring up at him with astonishment.

"Are you all right?" he heard himself asking.

She nodded her head, her eyes vacant and bewildered. Then he felt her hand reaching for him and he recoiled reflexively, standing and stepping away. Her eyes drew closed again and, for what seemed the longest time, he stood safely separated from her, struggling to say something conclusive.

For what he wanted, incredibly, in that obscene aftermath, was to be granted her understanding and forgiveness. Yet even in his drunkenness, or, perhaps, due to it, he recognized at last that Marcelline Tatia was not the one from whom he sought forgiveness and understanding. Indeed, Marcelline Tatia was little more than fuel for a fire that Hazzard had unconsciously constructed and ignited in order to project a monstrous shadow that would reveal once and for all to him the monster residing *within.*

Duly terrified—of himself—he left in silence.

Twenty-two

As he worked his way toward the black water of the Hudson, Hazzard found himself foundering in terror through the abandoned Penn Central railroad yard beneath the rusting iron trestles of the West Side Highway. He recognized that his terror issued from a new notion of his character so fundamentally at variance with his past conceptions that he could never again look upon himself with the same vain and complacent deceit. He had lived his entire life not to reach this earnest reckoning, but it was irreversible now, and the terror of its truth, which revealed him to be unloving, grasping, violent and friendless, ravaged him as viciously as any physical evisceration.

He stared across the black river to the cliffs of the Palisades. Somewhere out there, not more than thirty miles west, he'd been molded for nearly twenty years for manhood. All along the way, major and minor mistakes had been made, unto him and by him; and now he would have to work at re-forming himself.

Tears of remorse rose in his eyes and the hazy corolla of eerie light above the cliffs appeared aqueous. He felt himself to be drowning in his own illusions as he remembered how, as a young man, he had stared night after night from his bedroom window across the dreary Jersey flatlands to the menacing skyline of Manhattan. Back then he had believed such a city must be the very locus of his dream of a separate and salvational universe. But the thousand natural shocks of Experience had taught him otherwise; and he acknowledged now that it had been his dream, finally, that had broken him. For in his shamelessness and his shame, he had never dared to consider the degree of its desperation. The desperate do dumb things, and Hazzard had indeed dumbly dreamed that a place or a person could magically and passively save him from himself; and when Marcelline Tatia had failed to incarnate his dream, his reaction was to blame and nearly murder her. In fact, however, it had been the dreamer all along who was responsible for this nightmare.

This was the extent of his gnosis: *He* was responsible.

Yet who, after all, was he? And what was it that he sought unconsciously to obscure by fragmenting himself into a system of compensatory, antagonistic personalities? And was his true motivation to avoid himself by such fragmentation or to keep himself company from a loneliness inspired by his fear of others? Then again, perhaps, his most fundamental fear wasn't of others so much as of himself. If that were the actual case, then what about himself inspired such fear? Was it not, finally, a basic ambivalence about whether or not he loved or hated, himself no less than others? For had not the Boy and the Son, from their very epigenesis, been unable to agree on Hazzard's feelings about his mother and father; and later still, had not the allies of the Boy—the Mother, Recluse and Depressive—and the allies of the Son—the Father, Punk,

Actor and Paranoid—been similarly unable (or unwilling) to concur in their feelings for Hazzard himself? Indeed, had it not, somehow, devolved disastrously onto the Lover to dream that some lover, by loving him, might resolve Hazzard's ambivalence toward himself? Moreover, hadn't the Writer, in his grandiose fantasy that unconditional admiration for his work might overcome the anguish of Hazzard's abiding ambivalence about himself, only exacerbated ancient strategies of evasion and passive transcendence?

So now he had fallen, fortunately perhaps, from his dream into Experience. Fallen, he recognized that neither the Lover nor the Writer nor any of the other imaginary inhabitants of his head could magically resolve what was "his" mundane responsibility: namely, to accept life's mandate that his prideful dream of infinite possibilities for himself was indeed dead, and that a modest life of finite possibilities was not a nightmare. After all, he was constructed of flesh and bone—not of the stuff of dreams.

Opening his eyes to the river, an impulse arose in him to leap at once from the rotting promenade abutting the black water breaking below him against the rusted pilings. He imagined that the shock of the freezing water would drive him into unconsciousness in a matter of minutes, and that immediately thereafter the current would carry him downriver to deposit him, ingloriously dead, in the backwaters of Bayonne or Jersey City.

But how ridiculous he was in his rebellion! Leaning over the railing, he hung his head repentantly and, rather than leaping, simply sighed.

Later, turning his back on the vainest strategy of evasion dreaming has ever inspired, Jack Hazzard took a tentative, but conscious, first step in the direction of solid ground.

Twenty-tHree

HAZZARD spent the following day in bed with a hangover and a head cold. Drifting in and out of restless sleep, he woke at twilight to hear the Teacher within himself say solemnly, "If you bring forth what is within you, what you bring forth will save you; and if you fail to bring forth what is within you, what you fail to bring forth will destroy you." "I don't understand," said the Patient. "Then find a teacher," said the Teacher. "I thought you were the Teacher," the Son said. "The Teacher must have a teacher," the Teacher answered. "Is the Mother the teacher?" the Boy asked. "Or is the Father the teacher?" the Son inquired. "They are not the teacher," the Teacher said. "Is the analyst the teacher?" the Patient wondered. "The teacher is one who helps you bring forth what is within you," said the Teacher. "Aren't we all within?" said the Depressive. "You are within," answered the Teacher, "but you came from without." "That's right," said the Patient, "we're each introjections." "The teacher," said the Teacher, "is the one who brings forth that which is eternally within and has been obscured by that which has come from without." "I follow you," said the Recluse, remembering now certain of the Writer's readings in the esoteric. "He's just crazy," the Paranoid said of the Teacher. "Some mystical fanatic."

The Mother interrupted. "You'll be late for your appointment with your parents." "I'll shower and dress," said the penitent Son, whose displaced feelings had created such hell in Hazzard's Head.

But Hazzard went instead into the living room, where, blowing his nose, he searched through his shelves of books for a volume the Recluse vaguely remembered from Hazzard's student days. The Writer opened the book and located a section that was prominently underlined.

. . . One might call the despair now to be considered the despair of manliness. In connection with the kind just described it may be called: despair viewed under the determinant of spirit.

. . . The despair (previously described) was despair over one's weakness: the despairer does not want to be himself. But if one goes a single dialectical step further, if despair thus becomes conscious of the reason why it does not want to be itself, then the case is altered, then defiance is present, for then it is precisely because of this that a man is despairingly determined to be himself.

First comes despair over the earthly or something earthly, then despair over oneself about the eternal. Then comes defiance, which really is despair by the aid of the eternal, the despairing abuse of the eternal in the self to the point of being despairingly determined to be oneself. But just because it is despair by the aid of the eternal, it lies in a sense very close to the true, and just because it lies very close to the true it is infinitely remote. The despair which is the passageway to faith is also by the aid of the eternal: by the aid of the eternal the self has the courage to lose itself in order to gain itself. Here on the contrary it is not willing to begin by losing itself, but wills to be itself.

. . . In order to will in despair to be ourself there must be consciousness of the infinite self.

"Find a teacher," the Teacher intoned. "Listen!" said the Depressive petulantly, "I have enough trouble with the finite self, let alone the fucking infinite self." "What kind of grandiose crap is this anyway?" said the Patient. "The infinite self!"

The Teacher turned to the Son and rested his hands gently upon him. "Don't be afraid," said the Teacher. "Trust me." "I trust you!" exclaimed the Boy, pulling away from the Mother and running now to the Teacher, who asked, "Why do you trust me when all the others doubt me?" "Because," replied the Boy, "I've maintained the spirit of infancy well into adulthood." "The Writer's making him say that," protested the Father. "We're only playing," cried the Boy, skipping around wildly now, swinging his stuffed rabbit in his flailing arms. "Get dressed!" screamed the Mother; and the Father, standing helplessly with his hands in his pockets, beheld the mayhem in Hazzard's Head and muttered, "Ever since he stopped listening to me he's been completely out of his mind." "Just because I'm different than you," mumbled the Son resentfully—but he immediately fell silent when he noticed the Patient taking notes.

Hazzard showered and dressed, and, cloaking himself warmly in cap and coat, descended from his apartment into the snowy twilight.

The depth of accumulation surprised him: snow covered his ankles. "Great," complained the Paranoid, sneezing. "I'll be sick for a month." "A month," the Punk chided the Patient. "You've been sick for years!"

Hazzard noticed that the cabs were proceeding with unusual caution and that most of them, though empty, had turned on the Off Duty display. He elected to walk rather than ride the subway. Trudging southward, he squinted through the snow to the towering building where Marcelline lived.

"The least you could do," the Lover told the Actor, "would be to call and make sure she's all right." "Absolutely not," said the Patient. "The conflict is internal and she's irrelevant."

The mournful Depressive voiced no protest as the Son hurried Hazzard through the snow to toast the birthday of his father, whom the Patient had forced him not to see for nearly a year now. Dad! the Son thought, wishing Hazzard would hurry, the Writer slowing him down, musing upon the snow, always observing, searching for significances, never letting Hazzard just live, and so exhausting himself, the only real relief coming, consequently, from sex and booze, the Boy never allowed to play, the Patient astonished by the degree of internal pressure percolating within Hazzard.

Snowplows were working to clear Times Square, which, with its sudden explosion of neon, was eerily mesmerizing amid so much snow falling in swift and shifting slants through the immediate atmosphere's prismatic light.

"Why in God's name did we ever move to this city?" the Recluse wondered, as Hazzard, nearing the restaurant, walked west now along Forty-seventh Street.

"How can you write about anything if you live in this small town where nothing happens?" His father had asked, visiting Jack upstate.

"Jill and I live here, Pop."

"If you can make it in Manhattan," his father had said, "you can make it anywhere. This place is nowhere."

"I don't want to make it in Manhattan."

"Great! So what are you going to do? Live in this little town with Jill, writing stories and growing vegetables in a little garden?"

"What if I do?"

"What kind of life is this?"

"The kind that's none of your business."

"Don't get me wrong, Jack. If you're happy living in a little house growing a little vegetable garden in this little town—well, frankly, I envy you."

"A writer can write anywhere, Dad."

"Exactly my point."

"Which escapes me, I'm afraid."

"Why live in a little town like this? What are you going to write about—gardening?"

"What do you know about writing?"

"What do you?"

"More than you."

"Why not travel? I thought all writers traveled."

"To where?"

"I don't know. Paris. Rome."

"Writers don't do that anymore, Dad."

"Well, don't ask me. You're supposed to be the creative one."

"I was thinking of going to Key West. Jill says it's nice there."

"Key West," said his father skeptically. "Isn't that a place where fairies go in the winter?"

"I don't know. Fairies go everywhere, just like everybody else."

"Why don't you think of some place interesting?"

"Such as?"

"Don't ask me, for God's sake. You're the one who's supposed to have the big imagination."

"Do I have to *ask you* to rake the leaves?" castigated his father upon returning home from the shoe store to find Jack staring mutely out his bedroom window when he was thirteen.

"I was dreaming of traveling."

"Can't you dream of traveling while raking the leaves?"

"I guess."

"I guess you have a place in mind to travel to?"

"I guess."

"Well, don't make *me* guess."

"I was thinking of Los Angeles."

"Los Angeles! Los Angeles is like Atlantic City, only bigger and with Mexicans instead of blacks."

"I was only pretending to go there," said his son weakly.

"Good God," his father criticized, another time, "all you do is sit in your room and talk on the phone as much as a woman. Why don't you go somewhere with a friend? You do have a friend, don't you?"

"Mike."

"Other than the dog, smartass."

"I guess."

"Well, why don't you go somewhere with a friend?"

"Maybe I will," said his son, inspirited.

"Where are you going?" shrieked his mother, one sunny Saturday morning.

"Blaine and me are going to Philadelphia."

"Blaine and *I.*"

"You're going too?"

"You're not going anywhere, young man. I'm calling your father."

"Philadelphia!" said his father on the phone from the shoe store. "Philadelphia's worse than Newark, for crying out loud!"

"Why are you sitting in your room in the dark?" his father asked, home from the shoe store that evening. "I thought you were going to Manhattan."

"Blaine went by himself to Philly."

"So, you can't go to Manhattan by yourself?"

"I'm scared of Manhattan."

"Yo!" cried the Actor now in Hazzard's Head. "Get it together, we're here!"

Hazzard wiped his cowboy boots on the entrance mat and started into the restaurant.

"Maybe," the Depressive said hopefully, "the snow forced them to turn back." "My dad's not scared of snow!" said the Son, as the Patient recited, by way of a reminder to the Actor, words the Writer and Recluse had memorized long ago. " *'And I pray that I may forget/ These matters that with myself I too much discuss/ Too much explain/ Because I do not hope to turn again/ Let these words answer/ For what is done, not to be done again/ May the judgement not be too heavy upon us.'* "

Hazzard saw them now, his mother and his father. They were seated in the rear of the restaurant, adjacent to a pile of logs that burned brightly in the hollow encasement of a bricked fireplace. "Mommy!" cried the Boy, "Daddy!" cried the Son. And the Father said to the Mother, "So, that's who we're supposed to be!" "They look like a very nice couple to me," said the Mother. "Yeah," said the Punk venomously, *"Look like* is right."

Smiling, kissing them now, first his mother, then his father, turning his cheek to meet theirs, he sat across from them as ashes from the fireplace blew across the floor beneath them.

Hazzard noted that his mother had gained weight and that her hair was now fully gray, the once lustrous black completely erased by time. Inveterately nervous, she dissembled a smile while inhaling cigarette smoke. The Actor in her son was sensitive to the Actress in his mother. "Sad," said the Patient, observing her watching Hazzard, her eyes furtive, revealing sorrow and fear, rage and dependency. "Mommy!" cried the Boy, waving invisibly.

Seated beside her, his father (Dad) seemed smaller than Hazzard remembered. His brown hair had thinned and his blue eyes had faded in color and intensity, as if simply worn down by the predictability of the quotidian. "Dad!" cried the Son, reaching out in Hazzard's Head.

"When I'm as old as they," said the Depressive, "they'll be dead." "That's right," said the Teacher. "Mercy." "For whom?" asked the Patient.

Putting her hand nervously to her hair, his mother said, "Did you have trouble with the snow, dear?"

The Actor waited for his line.

"I like it," Hazzard said. "Makes everything seem like a dream."

"Well," his mother replied, "we certainly never dreamed it would continue like this when we started in today."

"We can always stay at a hotel," his father replied, eyes fixed on the dinner menu.

"Oh, no," his mother said. "You know how much I hate linens slept on by strangers."

"No wonder I never worried about you having an affair!"

When his father winked at Hazzard, the Actor forced a smile to disguise the Son's anger and the Boy's fear.

A waiter approached to ask Hazzard what he would be drinking.

"Hurry up, Jackie," said the Mother. "The waiter's wait-ing!" "I'm sorry," the Son said as Hazzard glanced furtively at his father's drink, the Punk suggesting, "Vodka, man. Straight up." "Isn't vodka a girl's drink?" the Paranoid in-quired, the Actor clearing his throat, Hazzard saying out loud finally, "Absolut on the rocks with a twist of lemon."

"La-de-da!" the Father teased the Son in Hazzard's Head.

"Try this," offered his father, reaching Jack his Scotch.

Hazzard declined with a wave of his hand, and the next thing he knew the waiter deposited the Absolut before him.

"Doesn't your mother look great?" his father said, the three of them touching glasses, his mother rummaging in her handbag for a new package of cigarettes.

"You look fine, Mom," he heard himself say.

"I mean for an old broad," his father said, "she's still the prettiest girl I know."

"You're such a liar," his mother replied, Jack lighting her cigarette and then his own.

"Not that age should matter," his father resumed, "be-cause just last week I read an article that claims a couple can have sexual relations into their nineties."

"Your father," his mother said, exhaling, "has a one-track mind."

"Of course," his father continued, "this assumes the part-ners are still attracted to each other."

"Some other time with all this, Dad," Hazzard said calmly.

"Yes," said his mother. "Just sit quietly."

"Boy oh boy," his father said. "I'm just damned if I do and damned if I don't around you two."

"Listen now, Jackie," his mother interjected, "I . . ."

"Jack, mom."

"What did I say?"

"You said Jackie," Mr. Hazzard said.

"I'm sorry, dear. It's just a habit of mine. You'll always be my baby, I'm afraid, and you'll only understand why when you're a mother yourself."

"I agree with you there, Mom."

"Listen, dear, I want you to promise me the lead role when they make that movie of your book. They are going to make the movie, aren't they?"

"I doubt it," Hazzard told her.

"Don't disparage yourself like that, dear. I'm quite sure it will get made."

"It's not a matter of disparaging myself. Most screenplays just never get produced."

"You never know," his father said, *trying*.

"And when it does get made," his mother went on, trying too, "I want the lead role. You promise?"

"You got it," Hazzard said, the Boy crying, "She's only playing!" waving to his mother from Hazzard's Head, wanting the Actor to have Hazzard tell her he still loved her like old times, when she was nice to him and he could hold and trust her, safe and warm.

"So," his father said, "how's your love life?"

"You're not still seeing that Italian call girl, are you?" his mother asked.

Hazzard sent smoke rings to the ceiling. "If memory serves, Mom, Dad was the one who wanted me to date call girls."

In the ensuing silence, Hazzard signaled to the waiter with a circular motion of his finger to bring another round of drinks.

Studying her son, Mrs. Hazzard, clearly stricken with resentment, said in a measured tone, "You have absolutely no right whatsoever to say such a thing about your father."

"It's all right," his father said. "I can take a joke."

"I demand you apologize," his mother whispered, Hazzard noticing the dementia flare momentarily in her chilly eyes.

"Please do forgive me, Pop," he said preposterously.

"Thank you," his mother replied, extinguishing her cigarette, her face averted while she constructed a mask of composure.

The new drinks arrived.

"Cheers!" Hazzard said, and they all touched glasses again.

"Now listen," his father said, working toward levity, "I don't care if you don't ever get married, Jack, but just give your mother and me a grandchild already, will you?"

"Would have," Hazzard said, the Punk flaring ungovernably, "but the abortionist has gotten to all three."

"I'm going to pretend I didn't hear that," his mother said, and his father withdrew in perplexity and chagrin, his hands disappearing.

"Irv," his mother said, "take your hands from your pockets and don't lean back in the chair."

Obeying her, his father said to Hazzard, "Fortunately with me it's in one ear and out the other."

"Let's call the waiter over," Hazzard said, "and I'll pick on him for a while."

"I'm not picking on your father," his mother said defensively and, leaning forward, whispered conspiratorially to her son, "You don't know everything, my dear. You don't know, for instance, that your father was in the hospital three months ago."

"What?"

"It was nothing," his father said, waving his hand dismissively.

"It wasn't nothing and we didn't even have a telephone

number where we could reach you because your old number had been changed and unlisted."

"What the hell happened, Dad?"

"It was nothing. I'm fine. I went in for a hernia operation. I aggravated the God damn thing beating the pants off your uncle on the tennis court!"

"One day you'll drop dead on that stupid tennis court," his mother said.

"Another drink?" Mr. Hazzard said, polishing off his second and pointing to his son's glass as he ordered another Scotch.

"Please," Jack said, drinking.

"You drink too much, Jackie."

"Jack, mom."

"I said Jack. Irv, didn't I say Jack?"

"I didn't hear. I was ordering the drinks."

"Anyway," his mother said, "I'm just grateful your father survived the Christmas season. Next Monday I'm taking him to Barbados for a week. Just look at the rings under his eyes, Jack. It's no secret he suffered terribly when you refused to speak with us. So, please, try not to do that again. Not for my sake, but for Daddy's. Because he's not going to live forev . . ."

"Really, Marion!" his father interrupted, not knowing what to do with his hands, and so folding them cautiously on the table before him.

"Just don't pretend you're so tough to impress Jack!" His mother turned to him, her son. "I'll have you know your father nearly choked to death on a peanut at the country club. And on the very day that Harold Gold dropped dead of a heart attack on the tennis court."

Hazzard thought for a moment that this was a bit of burlesque over which he was supposed to laugh; he was wrong.

"Harold Gold," his father said impatiently, "was a smoker. Two packs a day."

"First a hernia, Irv, then a choking attack, and *then* a coronary. Just like that I'll be a widow and pestering Jackie about when he's going to take his old and lonely mother out for a nice dinner."

"You just called him Jackie again," his father said.

"I'm his mother and I'll call him whatever I want. God knows he calls me worse things than Jackie in those books of his."

"What about that?" his father now asked him solemnly. "You don't poke fun at us again in this new one, do you?"

"Come on, Pop," Hazzard said. "You know my books are fictional."

"Which means what?" his father said, laughing nervously. "That you're free to make us look worse than we really are?"

"The new book's about child abuse," Hazzard said vaguely.

"Well," said his mother, "I certainly do wish you'd explain that to everyone at the beach club, the tennis club and the country club. Because they look at us, Jackie. They look at me especially. And I don't think it's right of them—or you, for that matter."

"I'm sorry my books cause you discomfort," Hazzard said. "Really."

Mr. Hazzard raised a finger to make a point.

"Why can't you write something nice about the family for a change?"

"Failure of imagination, perhaps," Hazzard said sardonically.

"That's not Daddy's point!" his mother interjected.

"Hey!" Hazzard said. "What is this, a trial or a birthday celebration?"

"It's a conversation," his father said, opening his hands. "Because, frankly, I always thought we were close, you and me."

The drinks arrived and Mr. Hazzard paused to work on his.

"Thing is, Jack," he went on, swallowing, "I loved you like crazy. That's what I've been thinking about ever since you refused to get together with us. Now your mother and myself, yes, we had a tough time when you were growing up. You don't know how sorry we are about that."

"I'm very sorry," his mother interposed, "but I have absolutely nothing to apologize for."

"Well," his father said, "I'm talking for myself here. So, yes, all right, I made mistakes. I'm sorry for those mistakes, Jack. I don't feel guilty about them, damn it, but I wish like hell it could have been different."

"You're drinking too much, Irv!"

His father ignored her.

"I don't like saying this, Jack, but I will. I'm going to. Frankly, for a while there I was set to leave your mom. It was touch and go there for a while, a long while, personally. Christ, it still is. But the point here is that you got caught in the crossfire. All right, it's that I'm sorry about. But the other point is how we all suffered. So what I hope you realize is how we always loved you back there, even if I didn't do such a hot job of showing it. I mean, who was I myself? A shoe retailer trying to live on twenty-five bucks a week."

"He's drunk," his mother said. "Do you hear him?" But there were tears in her eyes and she was holding her husband's hand.

Hazzard cleared his throat to whisper, "It's okay, Pop. I understand."

His father referred to his wristwatch. "We'd better order

our dinners if we want to make the curtain." And lifting his eyes quickly to his son, Jack Hazzard, who was lighting a cigarette, Mr. Hazzard winked stealthily before signaling the waiter and wrapping his arm around his wife's shoulder.

After dinner Hazzard watched his mother apply lipstick, her eyes fixed on the hand mirror before her.

"How's my lipstick look?" she asked him as his father pocketed the credit card receipt. Hazzard pivoted to remove his overcoat from the chair and heard his father say, "Very nice."

Then they went out together; and he kissed them goodbye at the corner. The snowfall had brought traffic to a halt and the silence was remarkable in the white night.

He watched them walk away, arm and arm, old now, laughing for some secret reason as the snow swirled about them. He was happy that they had laughed together, sliding away like dancers; happy that they were leaving, too.

In his momentary happiness, he found himself calibrating their increasing distance from him by counting the imprints their boots left in the snow—snow that was falling so swiftly now that by the time they had disappeared into the flurry of flakes, their path away from him had become fully obscured; so that even if the distance appeared infinite, in his heart he knew that they were closer that that—closer, somehow, than before, which was, perhaps, close enough.

Twenty-four

WHEN he reached his apartment, Hazzard undressed and prepared for sleep. For a moment he stared into the snowy night at the towering apartments twinkling with lighted windows, behind which, he imagined, others quite like himself must be staring at the world with the same dumb wonderment and exhilaration and anguish. This simple sense of solidarity wasn't much, but it would do; it would have to.

As he slid beneath the warm blankets, resting his head upon a pillow and clicking off the little lamp at his side, the phone rang once before the answering machine intercepted the call. Adjusting the volume dial, Hazzard heard the incoming message reveal to the darkness: "It's me, darling. I can't leave because of the snow. I wish you were in my bed. Call me."

Hazzard closed his eyes. Though several hours remained in the old year, he folded his hands upon his racing heart and, cheating a little, passed his New Year's resolution prematurely—eight to five.

That he experienced only a little consolation in his new resolve—well, perhaps this meant he'd become a man after all.

About the Author

Born in 1951, Scott Sommer was raised in New Jersey and educated at Ohio Wesleyan and Cornell universities. He has received a National Endowment for the Arts grant and a Creative Artists Public Service fellowship. He is the author of two novels, *Nearing's Grace* and *Last Resort*, and a collection of stories, *Lifetime*. Mr. Sommer lives in New York City.